Dedication

I would like to thank all of those who kept inspiring me throughout the writing of the stories in this book…my family who supported me, Lizzie Waterhouse -- my OCD inflicted publisher who kicked my ass to get this done and my friends who gave me feedback on my work. Thank you all again. I couldn't have done it without you!

I0684885

"When you grow up
you lose your
imagination...I refuse
to grow up!"

Unknown

Contents

Axe Murder Hollow

There is a place just outside of town. Once there was a house on that land, no not a house, a mansion. Sadly, that was years ago. Now it is an empty lot with just the remnants of the foundation and a flight of crumbling cement steps leading down to the original basement. Everything else is long gone.

The site is still very much occupied, though. Hundreds of teenagers hang out there drinking and smoking pot. If you just look down the hill, you can see a shack where a tribe of gypsies have settled in.

Those gypsies are friendly enough during the day. They will serve you food, tell your fortune and especially talk about the legend of the empty field and what happened there shortly after they moved in. However, at night they become extremely protective of the area even to the extent of chasing visitors away at gunpoint.

As the story goes, back in 1964 Dr.

Harold Barry was the owner of the property. As the town's only doctor, he was one of Allegheny Heights' richest and most respected citizens. He lived there with his wife Linda and their children, four year old Michael and Alex, who was twelve.

The Barrys attended the local church every week where Harold served on the board, and Linda sang in the choir. For their entire marriage, they never missed any church services, even when Linda was ready to deliver her children. She would be in labor and still attend services even if just for a few minutes before heading to the hospital.

"Yeah, we all knew the Barrys," the then mayor, Jonathon Tower said. "They were the pillars of the community. They attended church. They worked with the young people in town and they always helped out anytime anybody needed anything. All anyone had to do was ask, and the Barrys made sure they got it. Hell, there was a family who lost their home in a fire—a husband, wife and three kids. If I remember right Dr. Barry took them in; he fed them and gave them a home for over a year. The thing was, he never knew them before that night."

"If and when Dr. Barry had to leave

town for a conference or something like that, he would actually pay for a doctor to come from Pittsburgh or Cleveland to take care of his patients. He even brought a special pediatrician in for the kids from the Children's Hospital in Akron, Ohio in order to make sure the kids had the best care available. He and his wife paid for all of the medical bills for his patients while he was gone."

It was hard, if not impossible, to find anyone from that time who didn't paint the Barrys, especially Harold, as saints. The consensus was that Harold Barry would have been the Pope if it were up to the people of that small town.

The truth is that the town knew Harold Barry, but they didn't know Harold Barry. Oh, they knew that he had worked his way through medical school in a series of funeral parlors. What they didn't know is that he also operated a side business cremating bodies of people whose deaths someone didn't want anyone to know about. These ranged from deaths caused by accidents, to dogs and cats that parents brought in to keep the deaths from their little kids or by people who made a living out of other people's misery.

After graduation, he tried to quit, but

his "clients" wanted him to keep working for them. He was living outside of Pittsburgh at the time; he wasn't married and wasn't even seeing anyone. So, with the promise of good money and lots of work from his professional clients, he rented a warehouse, and a few weeks later, set it up as a crematorium. For a time, he kept both, this business as well as his medical practice going. After a while, he decided to shut down his office and crematorium and moved to a small town to set up a new medical practice.

Once there, he met and married Linda, and he bought the house they raised their family in. But the money in a small town wasn't that good, so he built an extra room under the basement and opened a pet crematorium. For years, it worked out well for the doctor, but then it happened...his old clients found him and started pressuring him to work for them. Of course, he refused. But they made sure he knew what would happen if he didn't, and that involved his wife and kids.

A few days later, Harold agreed, and he was back in business. The room where he did this sinister work was brightly lit, but the unfinished stone walls and the un-cremated bodies made it look like something out of a horror movie. There was a large exhaust fan that sucked the smell and the fumes from the room, expelling them to a vent on the other side of the hill next to the Barry house. It wasn't quite the professional setup he had in Pittsburgh, but it suited his needs.

Within a couple of weeks, Harold was spending his weekends down in that room taking care of business. As distasteful as it was for the doctor, it was very lucrative. Each body he cremated made him and his family an extra $5,000. The money didn't do much to calm his uneasy feelings, but it helped, especially when he was able to renovate part of the house and put in a new home theatre system which included a room just off of the living room with a 100-inch projection TV.

Not anyone, not even Linda, knew what was below the basement, even though she used the basement daily for laundry and other household chores. He had told her it was just a pet crematorium and nothing more. She believed him. After all, he was her husband, and he wouldn't lie to her.

A diary page found after the house was gone spoke volumes about what Harold was thinking. "There were so many bodies... I could not believe how many people they killed for any reason. One of them, a boy about eighteen, was killed because he couldn't pay them a hundred dollars he had borrowed. Why would anyone do that? I have to get out of this...get away from them before they come after Linda and the kids."

For months, he continued his work. Between the pets and the bodies coming in, the oven was running twenty-four hours a day from Friday evening through Sunday night when Harold shut it down to sleep. The bad thing was that the bodies just kept coming. Coming from hundreds of miles away to just down the block; there were always more.

Then it started. Linda would be in the kitchen and pans would fly from their hooks and crash to the floor, the TV would change channels or just turn on and off on its own, and there would be the sounds of someone walking at all times of the day and night. Sometimes it sounded like the clopping of work boots, at other times it was the click click of high heels. Sometimes it would be single footsteps, other times it was as if numerous people were walking around in the house. It was becoming extremely annoying.

"Why is this happening to us?" Linda asked one night when things were particularly noisy. "This was such a pleasant house when we moved in. Why would it suddenly appear to be haunted?"

Harold thought for a minute. He knew he couldn't tell the truth. "Maybe it's spirits from years ago. Perhaps there was a settlement or something here when the area was first established. It's possible that there were people who lived here and their spirits have returned, but there is no way to know for sure. I doubt that they kept records back then."

"Well, I'm going to check it out tomorrow," Linda said. "There has to be something somewhere maybe down at city hall or the historical society. There HAS to be something." She emphasized the word "has" to the point where Harold jumped back in shock. "There has to be some record somewhere." Harold knew better than to argue, so he just agreed and went back to his business.

The rest of that night was even more active than usual. Pictures flew across the room, dishes smashed in the kitchen, and Linda was slapped across the face a couple of times. Once she was slapped so hard that it left a mark and she was found crumbled on the floor crying.

She cried out to Harold, but he thought

she was exaggerating and he told her to go bed and forget about everything. Finally, after almost an hour, his temper was just about at its limit with her talking about the ghosts. "Damn it Linda, there's no such thing as ghosts," he screamed. "I don't give a damn what that TV show says. It is all in your mind, and that is that. I don't want to hear anymore!"

"You don't know what you're saying!" she yelled back. "They're real, they're here, and they're after us!"

"Linda," he shouted back. "I want you to stop talking like that and get to bed … Now!"

"Fine," she screamed as she started down the hallway.

Although she was upset, Linda decided that it wasn't worth arguing. She knew what she knew, and there wasn't going to be any changing of that. She went upstairs, grabbed a pillow and blanket and put them outside the bedroom door. She then went back in, locked the door behind her and did what her husband had suggested…she went to bed. A few hours later, Harold went up the stairs to the bedroom and tried to get in. But she wouldn't open the door, so he unwillingly took the blanket and pillow and moved back to the living room where he settled down for the night.

The next morning, Linda was the first to wake up. She was still furious, so she didn't bother waking Harold up. She just got dressed and went for a walk. At the end of the driveway, she was stopped by the old Gypsy woman who lived next door.

"Honey," she said, "you have to get out of that house, there are many there who wish to do you harm. They have died sad, meaningless deaths, and they are angry. That house is where their anger is centered. You have to leave."

Linda just looked at her, speechless. She knew that what the old woman was saying was true, but there was no possible way she could leave. By the time she gathered herself together, the old woman was gone, and she was standing there all alone. She thought for a minute and then continued her walk, ending up at the coffee shop in town where she drank a few cups of coffee before returning home.

As soon as she walked in the door, she went over to the sleeping Harold and shook him so hard that he nearly fell to the floor.

"What in the hell?" he muttered.

"I want to know right now what you have been up to and don't try telling me some bullshit," she said. "If I think you are lying, I am going to take the kids and leave, and you will never see any of us again."

"Hon," he started, "you know I cremate animal remains after I get home from work."

"Yeah," she responded.

"Well..." he said without finishing.

"Well what?" she demanded to know.

"Well, business has been really good lately," he said. "I have been doing some outside work for people who want relatives cremated, and that's it! I promise you that."

"Are you sure?" she asked. She was still pissed when she heard a scream come from the boys' room.

Harold and Linda both ran down the hallway. The bedroom door was closed, and Harold didn't stop to open it. He just smashed through it with all the force he could muster. Once the dust had settled and he got his bearings, he saw a figure. There, standing over his sons, was a man wearing ragged, bloody clothes. He wasn't doing anything, he was just standing there looking down at the boys.

"Who the hell are you?" Harold yelled as he rushed into the room.

The man didn't say a word. He didn't even look up. He just stared down at the boys.

Suddenly the person raised his arms and one of the boys let out another horrific scream. A second later Harold noticed that his sons were staring into space, their faces frozen in a grimace that made the Joker look like a Miss America. He gasped when he saw that their night clothes were covered in bright red blood...fresh blood. Harold knew that it was fresh because he could see it squirt out from freshly cut veins and arteries.

Linda got to the door shortly after Harold, and he grabbed her and would not let her enter the room. He didn't tell her anything. He just forced her back down the hallway and into the living room. He lowered her into a chair and told her to stay put until he got back. She was in shock, and so confused she didn't say anything. She just sat there just like she was told.

Harold went back to the bedroom and saw that the man was gone. Harold must have stood there for an hour, just staring into the room. His children still lay in their beds, which were now covered with blood, as was the floor and the walls. He walked over and looked into his dead sons' eyes. He told each of them that he was sorry, and he covered them with fresh sheets from the closet. As he left, he closed the smashed door and walked back down the hallway.

He was crying uncontrollably. He had no idea what he was going to tell his wife, but he knew he had to tell her something. It took him a long time to walk that twenty feet back to the living room, but it had to be done.

He did not want her to see him crying, it would bring out that he didn't want to answer.

He stepped through the door and into the living room when suddenly he felt a sharp pain to the right side of his head.

As he fell to the floor, he heard Linda's voice, "I know what you did you son-of-a-bitch." She was screaming at him, but her voice didn't sound like anything Harold had heard before. "I know you brought this on us! How could you think I wasn't going to find out?"

He grabbed the side of his head as he tried to stand up. He could tell that it was bleeding and bleeding hard. "What are you talking about?" he asked as his vision clouded over.

"He told me what you've been up to." Her voice was getting angrier and angrier.

"Who told you what?" Harold asked.

Linda pointed over at the corner of the room near the front door. Harold struggled to look as he stood up. There, he saw the man from the boys' bedroom standing and staring back at him.

"Who is...?" Harold started to ask as he fell into unconsciousness.

Linda watched as the man walked over to Harold and began to stab him over and over again. He stabbed him once for the body of every innocent person he had cremated over the years. Harold's body quivered every time the knife went in. In the distance, Linda could hear a faint laugh as if someone was enjoying the justice they never had in life.

As soon as the body stopped moving and the laughter ceased, the man walked over to Linda and said that he only did what he had to do and that he had no regrets and neither should she. Just before he faded from view, he reassured her that she would see her children again in another life. Then he faded from view leaving her all alone with the bodies of her family in an otherwise empty house

She didn't say a word. Not that it would have done any good if she had. There was no one left to hear it.

She walked out to the kitchen, blew out the pilot lights to the stove, turned on the gas and went back into the living room. Once there, she turned on the gas to the fireplace and went to the other side of the room, lit a candle and sat down. There was a small radio sitting next to her, so she turned it on to some disco station at an Ohio college. And then she took a nap.

According to neighbors, the fire started about an hour later. Actually they said that it started out as an explosion that rocked the entire valley, and then came the flames. Some say the house only burned for a couple of hours, others said it burned for three days before anyone could get close enough to find anything out.

Once the fire department made it in, they sifted through the ashes, but no bodies, or any traces of any bodies were ever found. The only thing left was the stairway to the basement and the foundation of the house. Nothing else.

The only other thing left is a legend. It is said that, on a summer evening, you can see pairs of glowing eyes floating around the property. Some say that it is the eyes of the victims of Harold Barry's oven and the members of his family who died needlessly for his crimes. Others say that the "eyes" are just mating fireflies, but no one knows for sure and the gypsies, who still reside next to the property, aren't talking. That may be the best thing, don't you think?

Hellstrom

My name is Allen. Don't bother asking me about my last name; I don't think I ever had one. I was born in a human breeding farm out in Essex County and, as soon as I was born, I was taken and placed in a school called Hellstrom Academy.

I had nurses taking care of me all day and all night. That, I learned from some of the other kids. But, as I grew older, I could see that this was the perfect place for a baby to be raised. They played classical music all the time, and the nurses made sure that no baby ever cried for more than thirty seconds before they took care of any need the baby might have. When I heard that, I realized how lucky I was to be raised in such a place.

The first thing that I really remember was the year of my fifth birthday. Everyone born that year was removed from the dorms we shared while we were younger. I was one of the first to go. I remember being taken to a room with a nurse who came over and comforted me. She played with me for a little while and then I was taken into a room filled with doctors and other nurses. "Allen," one said, "just relax and you'll be done in a few minutes."

I was relaxed. Why shouldn't I be? I was always treated well. Why would this be any different? Another nurse came and removed my trousers and laid me on a small bed. She had a needle in her hand and she told me that I would feel a little pain and then I wouldn't feel anything. She placed the tip of the needle against my groin and slid it into my skin very gently. She was right, there was no real pain. Then a doctor came over to me, and a few seconds later, I was walked out of the room and into another where I was told to rest. But, before I was allowed to lie down, the nurse injected something into my wrist. That hurt worse than whatever it was that they did before. But I was a big boy and didn't cry...even though I really wanted to.

During the time we were at Hellstrom, we were ostracized by a lot of the kids who went to school there, I found out why, when I was sixteen. Most of the students attending were from the upper-crust families of the area; their parents paid a lot of money for their kids to attend school there. Those of us who lived there, on the other hand, were clones created from drug addicts, homeless people and prostitutes from around the country. They were paid fifty pounds for their cells and then sent packing. That bothered some of us, but there wasn't anything we could do about it, so we just accepted it and went on with our lives.

Now, I had two friends back then— Jessica was one of them, and Stew was the other. They were the same age as me, so were brought into the room within a couple minutes after I was and they both got the same shots that I did. We were allowed to rest for a couple of hours, then Stew and I were taken to a room that we would share until we turned eighteen. Jessica was taken to another building. Stew and I assumed that she was placed with the girls, but we weren't sure.

Occasionally, once we got a little older, they would let us go into town. It was on these excursions that Stew and Jessica started building a relationship. It was something special that seemed to develop just between them. At the same time, the three of us stuck together.

Sadly, we were separated when we hit our eighteenth year. I was sent to Southampton, Stew went to Embelton, and Jessica went to St. Ives. Before we left, however, we were told why we were born, and our purpose in life, and that was to become a Cara...short for carrier. We were to travel the country making sure to visit the farm communities and try to become infected with various diseases. In our twentieth year, if we survived, we were to be used as organ donors for the upper classes in the major cities...especially royalty.

We were given stipends from the government to live on. Mine was a little over 500 pounds a month, which meant that I was poor, but better off than a lot of others who were jailed for living on the streets.

I heard stories of Caras living through two or three donations. By that time, however, they were usually drained and barely alive. I thought that they looked like zombies, but they were alive and that was good enough. There were a few who died during their first donations and a rare few who lived long enough to make it to their fourth donation. By that time, they were not released—none of us were ever released. Instead, they were locked in a room and starved to death, which didn't take long because they were nothing but walking skeletons anyway.

Stew was the first of my friends to make a donation. If I remember right, he donated his right lung to some rich woman who was fifty-seven years old and spent her entire life smoking pot and drinking. Stew's lung was her fourth transplant. The big thing was that Stew came through it fine and was back to normal in just a couple of weeks.

Jessica got the next call. Her first "job" was to donate her fallopian tubes and uterus to some twenty-five-year-old who was unable to have kids. I guess the doctors either forgot or didn't know that we were sterilized when we were kids, but she was told that she had to do it, so she did as she was told.

As for me, for some reason, I wasn't given the message to take my place as a donor. Yeah, I gave blood on a fairly regular basis so that the antibodies I developed when I was a kid could cure some really nasty diseases. Thinking back, I remember being with dying people who suffered from things like plague, AIDS and so many other diseases that I could not remember all of them. For some reason, however, I never caught any of the diseases I had been exposed to and neither did any of the others I was with.

Jessica one time caught the flu from someone she was with, and everybody treated her like a leper until she recovered. But for those two weeks, Stew and I spent every moment with her including sleeping in beds that were pushed next to hers. We got the germs alright, but we never got sick—not in the least.

I heard that Stew had his second donation. It was one of his kidneys this time. It went to a woman who should have died. She was seventy years old and was living on tubes, but her husband paid for the kidney, so Stew gave it up. He had trouble after that one. He had to use a walker and carry a tank of oxygen with him at all times. That lasted a little over a month until he had his third donation.

I was watching through a window as the doctors administered the anesthesia. He looked at me and smiled just before he went under. They removed half of his liver. I didn't know who it was for, and I didn't really care. They made the initial incision and two minutes later, the liver was on its way to the next room. Suddenly, every alarm in the room started going off at the same time. Stew started to wake up. The first thing he did was look at me. There was a tear running down his cheek as he took a deep breath and then his soul left his body. The doctors didn't try to revive him. They just turned off the machines and walked out of the room. Stew was left there uncovered and all alone. But for him at last, the torture of making donations was over.

Me and Jessica got together a couple weeks later. She hadn't heard about Stew. When I told her, she broke down crying, and she was crying hard. I didn't know it at the time, but, despite the fact that I was in love with her, she had strong feelings of love for Stew. In fact, they had loved each other ever since they were friends when we were kids. I knew it was a bad time, but even so I told her how I felt about her, and she smiled. She was actually happy about it and, of course, that made me happy. Then she told me why.

There were always rumors that floated around Hellstrom, but ninety-nine percent of them weren't true. She told me that one she heard *was* true and that was that if two Caras got married they would be given a few extra years together just to be able to spend some time as a couple before they started giving donations "That would be for us," she said with a smile. So we went into town the next day, got a marriage license and were married. Then, we headed off to Hellstrom to get our forbearance.

It took us three days to get to Hellstrom by train and bus. When we got there, we saw so many young people who were just like we were, each of them learning that their lives would be in total service to the grasping rich. They all smiled at us as we walked by. We smiled back, but inside, our hearts were breaking for them—especially the littlest ones.

We had called ahead, so the director of Hellstrom was waiting for us at the entrance to the building. She hugged us and gave a welcome that we never expected. She was happy to see us so she wrapped her arms around us. But before we could say a word, after telling her about our marriage, she told us what we didn't want to hear. The forbearance was just a myth, and we were being sent back to the places that they had assigned us. We just thanked her and left. Yes, we were disappointed, but we weren't done yet.

I thought for a moment. I remembered that I had seen people coming and going to France on a regular basis. "Jessica," I said, "don't ask questions, just come with me. She did as I said, and we headed to Southampton where we boarded a ship to the mainland. I had heard that the French didn't have the

Caras program there so we could live out our lives happy and free from donations.

We settled in a little town on the French coast and lived there for more than twenty years. During that time, we ran into a few Hellstrom "graduates." I guess they had heard about how we got away and they did the same thing. Eventually, we met a nineteen-year-old girl who told us the best news we ever thought we could hear: Hellstrom was closed by the British government because of the cruelty they were inflicting on kids in the Caras program. This came about after there had been a rash of deaths in the complex. All of the rest of the kids were adopted to good families and were living happy lives.

We sat and cried, and we both said the same thing:"It was too bad Stew didn't live to see this." We both knew that he was happy at the news no matter where he was and that he would have been holding a party to celebrate. That was just the kind of guy he was, and we both loved and missed him for it.

The Day The Dragons Saved The Unicorns

In the northern part of Agoria was a valley. It has never been on any map, and very few humans ever wandered through the forests that covered the valley floor and spread up onto the sides of the surrounding mountains. Because of its isolation, many of the creatures that modern man consider mythological have survived and thrived.

The most numerous were the unicorns. Their numbers soon grew due to the isolation of the land. There were at one time around a thousand adults and nearly as many babies.

The last humans to visit this unicorn's habitat were hunters from the local farms, who were hunting for meat to feed their families.

Oft times, they would spend weeks or even months searching the valley for animals that were suitable for food.

In desperate times, like when snow covered the area for weeks, they would eat their cows and pigs. But when things got really bad, they often killed and ate their prized horses. When the horses were all dead, the local wildlife and birds were hunted to fill the need. Once the local wildlife was exhausted, they had to go to even more extreme measures, which meant spreading out to find food.

A small pass was found in between two mountains during one of those hard times. The pass was just barely big enough for a small man to fit through, but the hunters knew that they needed food to for their now starving families, so they explored every possibility. When they entered the pass, they found themselves in a plush valley.

The hunters thoroughly covered the area, but all they could find that matched anything they knew they could use as food were the unicorns. They were mostly interested in the female unicorns since it was thought that their meat would be more tender and more flavorsome. There were only a few taken at a time, but because of the hunting, the unicorn population was soon on the decline.

On one trip, the hunters killed a dozen of the unicorns. They were hauled back to the farms, cut up and served for their meals for more than a month.

On the last trip, a group of hunters cornered a herd of unicorns against the side of a sheer cliff. They aimed their crossbows at three of the females in the herd. There was a panic within the herd and the unicorns' screams could be heard throughout the valley.

The hunters pulled their bows back and, when they released, all three of the unicorns fell. However, not being satisfied with their kill, they reloaded and aimed again.

Before they could shoot a second time, they heard something in the distance—a roar that sounded more like the eruption of a volcano than the sound that an animal might make.

As the men looked around to see where the sound came from, the sky began to darken. They looked up and saw several dragons circling in the air above them. Barely above the treetops they flew, their eyes stared down at the hunters who stood in fear beneath them. In one quick movement, a large black dragon landed between the hunters and the unicorns.

Spreading its massive wings, it completely shielded the unicorns. Its eyes were locked on the men, following every move they made. A second later, while the other dragons circled above, the black dragon raised his head and shot blue flames into the sky.

The hunters, in pure panic, ran screaming back into the pass, heading home without their kill.

The black dragon followed them growling and spitting fire as it moved. As soon as the men rushed into the pass, the dragon stopped and looked at the rocks surrounding the opening. It let loose with a horrendous growl as if it was issuing a warning to the hunters.

Just then, all of the dragons landed around the first one. They looked at each other as if they were communicating. The black dragon stared down at the pass. It growled again, and all the other dragons followed suit. Suddenly each dragon opened it massive mouth, and blue flames covered the pass.

They were not trying to kill the men who had already made it through. Instead, their combined heat melted the surrounding rock and fused it over the entrance.

That was the last time a human could

ever invade the valley. It may have been fear, or it may just be the stories that became fairy tales created to scare children into behaving, but no one ever went to that pass again. Until this day the animals in that valley live peacefully and are there if anyone has the nerve to go and look.

I Survived The Little Bighorn

I don't know how I lived so long, but it has been a good life. I have lived, loved, drunk too much and been shot a couple times, but hell, that was the life I chose. Now, I have a secret that is sixty some years old. Since I'm counting down the days until I meet my maker, I figure that it's time to let people know all about it. My name is not the one everybody calls me by. I am, or was, Capt. Gerald H. Trenton. I served with the Seventh Calvary at the Little Bighorn and I was the one who escaped when the fighting started.

I was transferred into the Seventh on June 14, 1876. It wasn't a bad duty. I had three square meals a day, I didn't have to live in the barracks and my horse was well cared for. I brought my nineteen-year-old wife and our daughter out to Montana with me. That was one of the benefits of being an officer...you were able to have your family with you in the fort. Kitty got along fine once she was settled and starting hanging out with the other wives in the fort.

The days were hard. Custer made us get up at 5:00 a.m. to do calisthenics, practice marching and shooting practice, and that was all before breakfast. The rest of the morning was spent taking care of the horses. In the afternoons, there were patrols, more marching and more shooting practice. Lights out was at 7:30 p.m. and, except for some parties on the weekends, we were all in their quarters and asleep by 8:00.

I made it a point every morning to take Buck, my horse, out for a ride. That was fun because I usually went out of the fort. There were always Lakota Sioux Indians perched on the ridges watching me. A couple times, one or two of them would come down and talk to me. It was usually because they were hungry. Sometimes, they just wanted to be friendly. After a couple days, I began taking small bits of food with me and I was pleased to share it with them.

Soon, they weren't just people who were wandering the hills...they came to be my friends. Occasionally, they brought me blankets, moccasins and toys for Kitty and my daughter. Obviously, I had to hide these gifts when I got back to the fort. I would sneak them in hiding in my saddle bags and only take them out when I got into my quarters.

The last time I took one of my rides, Kitty went with me to enjoy the summer sun. Thinking back now, the date was June 24th. When we got out of the wagon to sit for a while, relax and enjoy the day, an Indian maiden walked over the hill and sat down with us. Her name was Flowing River but I just called her River. I really liked that name and it seemed to fit her. This day, she had a message for me

"Blue Eyes," she started, "do not leave the fort tomorrow. The elders have found the body of one of our warriors in the forest down by the river." I asked her to tell me more so she continued, "Tomorrow the elders have declared that our people will seek revenge for his death and many others. They say that they will fight the white men down at the river in a place we call the Greasy Grass. Tȟatȟáŋka Íyotake said that the mists have foretold of a victory for our people."

"Who is Tȟatȟáŋka Íyotake?" I asked.

"You know him better as Sitting Bull, the chief and father of our nation," River replied. "You have been a friend to our people and we do not wish you harmed." She looked around, almost as if to see if anyone was watching. "Please be careful Blue Eyes." With that she got up, without saying another word and ran over the hill.

"Kitty, we have to get back," I said as I stood up and took her by the arm. "I must report this to the colonel." We both got into the wagon and, with a crack of the whip, we started back. But this time the horse wasn't just walking. I kept pushing until he was at a full gallop.

The sun was at its summit when we made it back to the fort. I dropped Kitty off in front of the house and headed for headquarters. I was stopped at the door by Captain Keogh, the battalion commander. "What's the rush boy?" he asked. I explained what was told to me. The second I finished, he escorted me directly into Major Reno's office and they both escorted me into Custer's office.

"George," Reno said to Custer, "do you know of any of our soldiers killing an Indian in the past few days?"

"There hasn't been any action in the past

week," Custer replied. "Why?"

Major Reno tapped me on the shoulder and told me to repeat everything I had been told...and he meant everything. I told them about sharing my food with the Indians I had met and getting to know them. Of course this pissed Custer off to no end. "Continue," he said with a look that meant I would be lucky if I left his office alive. I looked at him. Yes, I was afraid and I had every right to be. I had been fraternizing with the enemy and that was grounds to be shot by a firing squad.

"I took my wife for a ride out of the fort," I said. "An Indian woman came over the hill. She told us the Lakota, Northern Cheyenne and Arapaho were planning an attack in the morning to seek revenge on the killing."

"Where is this attack supposed to take place?" Custer asked. When I told him the Little Bighorn, Custer looked disgusted and angry at the same time. "Do you expect me to take the word of a dirty Indian woman?" he said. "I can't base my decisions on what neither you or some Indian tell me. We will go on patrol tomorrow." He looked at Reno. "You take some of the troops off to the north. Take Benteen and his troops, too. I want you to be my backups."

After he finished with that, I was arrested but I was not removed from duty. I was ordered to march with Custer's battalion.

The night went faster than anyone thought it would. Reno told everyone what the plan was and there were more than a few who believed Custer was a bigger fool than we actually thought he was. When 5:00 came, we were, for the most part, already awake. We got dressed, ate a biscuit for breakfast, mounted our horses and started for the Little Bighorn River.

The sun was barely above the horizon when we left. But, by the time we reached a hill overlooking the river, the sun was high and bright and the temperature had risen to just about seventy-five degrees.

Custer, Reno and Benteen dismounted and walked to the edge of the crest. I was a little ways behind them, but I could see what they were seeing. Down in the valley were maybe fifty Indians huddled around a fire. It looked as if they were cooking lunch, but I couldn't be sure. "That isn't bad," Custer said. "It should take about ten minutes to take care of them all." Then he told Reno and Benteen to hold back and just take notes about the event.

41

I was just a captain, but I knew that, with all of the Indian nations involved, it was not going to last just ten minutes. It was going to be bloody and it was going to last a very long time.

Custer looked back at me. He had an expression that seemed to be saying he would be happy if I died in the battle. "Mount," was the only thing he yelled as Reno and Benteen took their men toward the north. Then he looked back at me again. "Trenton, you stay with me!" That meant that I was to be by his side for the entire battle.

Custer was the first to order his troops into the valley. Like he said, fifty Indians shouldn't be too much trouble. The problem was, I was right. As we rode into the valley more Indians appeared on horseback and started toward us. We were ordered to shoot to kill.

I had my rifle ready and loaded. We rushed through the valley with the Indians coming at us from the other end. I'm not sure who fired the first shot, but the sound echoed across the valley. And when it did, most of the warriors from the three nations came tearing their way directly at us. I looked toward a ridge at the other end of the valley and there was Sitting Bull watching the action.

It wasn't long before we were literally surrounded by a mass of Indians. Custer ordered us to dismount and engage. As ordered, I stayed within feet of Custer.

All around us, both Indians and soldiers were falling—one after the other. There were three soldiers killed for every Indian that fell. I could hear the arrows and bullets fly all around me as I hid behind my horse. Some got so close that I could feel a breeze as they passed. I was aiming, but I could not bring myself to shoot any of the Indians. Custer noticed this and he threatened to shoot me, until other things took his attention.

Sitting Bull was still up on the ridge watching the men below being massacred. Then I noticed that he was paying special attention to me. After a few minutes, he raised his arm and two of the warriors came riding at me at a full gallop. Each one grabbed an arm and lifted me off of the ground. I had seen that before. It usually meant that whoever was the unfortunate one to be captured in that manner was usually tortured or killed when they got back to the Indian village. Custer saw what was happening and he tried to shoot at the Indians, but they were too fast and he was too busy to get a decent shot.

I was in pain the entire way. It felt as if my shoulder was being ripped out of its socket...as a matter of fact I was sure that it was. After about twenty minutes of being dragged, I found myself in the Indian village.

I noticed that there were no men in the village, just women and children. I guessed that all of the men were back at the Little Bighorn. I was tied up and promptly taken to a tent that was full of furs. "Stay," I was commanded. I did manage to look outside and the two warriors who had brought me in were standing guard outside.

Off in the distance, I could hear the sound of repeating rifles. I knew, because of that sound, that the battle was going to be over quickly and I knew, once again because of the sound, that the Indians were going to be the victors. The soldiers were issued revolvers and single shot rifles and the Indians had the newer repeating rifles. I know that it was wrong, but Custer rolled the dice and lost.

A few minutes later, a couple of soldiers from Reno's company were brought in with me. They looked as if they had been beaten and were left nearly half dead. Then the rifle fire stopped, but I could still hear the screams of the dying and the war cries of the victors. Maybe an hour later, even those sounds stopped. There was a silence broken only by the cries of the babies in the camp. Hearing those sounds was worse than anything I had heard up to that point. It broke my heart. Luckily I knew my baby and wife were safe in the fort.

Soon, I heard the sound of running horses. It was faint, but it was there—hundreds of horses coming from the Little Bighorn valley. The Indians and Sitting Bull were returning and it was so easy to think that I was going to be killed for the amusement of the Indians who had tasted blood earlier. Then, after a couple minutes, I heard the voice of Sitting Bull call for his warriors to bring me out to face him. My arms were still tied behind me and the gag still in my mouth. I swear it was made from a buffalo's testicle, but who knew.

"You are the one called Blue Eyes?" Sitting Bull asked as he looked down on me.

"I am Blue Eyes," I mumbled in response through the foul tasting gag.

Sitting Bull raised his head and said something that I did not understand but suddenly my arms were untied and the gag was removed. I stood there too afraid to speak, sit or even move. Finally, I repeated my answer, "I am Blue Eyes, friend of Flowing River."

"I know who you are," he said putting his hand out to me. "You have helped many of my brothers. Flowing River talks well of you."

"Sitting Bull, I am a person...your nation are all people," I said as he smiled at me. "We are all brothers and sisters and that is what I believe." The chief must have been impressed because he called me to stand directly in front of him.

"Blue Eyes, you are truly a brother to the Indian," he said. "This mark will protect you and your children and their children from all of the nations who fought today." With that, he reached down, picked up a burnt out ember from the fire and stroked it across my forehead. It was still hot and it burned my skin in addition to making a black mark. He looked at me and smiled again. "Now Blue Eyes, return to your people. Tell them of my hatred of what has happened and my wishes that it will never happen again."

With that, I was escorted from the camp and pointed in the direction of my fort and send me on my way.

Before I hiked over the first ridge, I

heard the screams of the two soldiers they had brought in. I didn't know what the Indians were doing to them, but I could imagine. The sounds were something I would never forget.

When I was about two miles from the fort, I could see the flag at half-mast in mourning for the soldiers who didn't make it back. I must have sat there for an hour just crying. Then I thought...how can I go back to the fort? So, I waited and watched. Later I learned I survived the battle because of my friendship with Flowing River and her people and no one else did.

Later that night, I found my way into the fort, stole a horse and took off for the north. I knew that my wife and child would remember me as a hero when I was nothing of the sort. I wasn't a coward, but then I wasn't a hero either.

It is now the turn of the century. I'm old and I have decided to write this and leave it for my daughter before I die. I hope that she will understand what happened and how it happened and maybe, if my wife is alive she will share this story with her. I never meant to hurt them, but it is better this way. I just hope that they can forgive me!

Mission to Mars

DAY 1

APRIL 2, 2037

ENTRY 1

13:52:35

I cannot believe my luck. I am the first person to travel to Mars and back. I was told that they had developed a new engine that will make me go faster than any person from Earth had ever gone. I should make it to Mars in about a month, circle it a couple of times and then be back here in time for the 4th of July. Won't that be great? The problem is, I will miss Easter. It is little Laurie's first one, and I would really love to be there to share it with her, but I should be far from Earth by the time Easter comes along. I left her a recording on the computer telling her how much I love her and how much I miss her. I just hope that her mom will read it to her.

Well, it's almost time to launch, so I have things to do. I sure hope that this goes well.

ENTRY 2

17:23:01

Lift off went as expected. They can simulate all they want, but there is nothing that will train you for the stress and the sounds of lift off. I am now in orbit 564 miles from Earth, and traveling at roughly 18,000 miles per hour. Great Britain, Germany, Russia and China have flown by the window in the last twenty minutes. No one who doesn't come up here will believe how beautiful our planet is. I have two days to orbit Earth before I start the trip to Mars. God, I hope I can see my house when I fly over it. I know that I can't, but it is nice to imagine that I can.

DAY 3

APRIL 4, 2037

05:15:45

ENTRY 1

Today is the day! I just got off a talk with Mission Control. Everything is going fine, and the burn is set to take place at 05: 45:12. That gives me a half hour to get my last look at Earth for some time to come. I can see a hurricane starting up in the Atlantic. I sure hope it doesn't hit Florida too hard. This will be the first one that my family will go through without me there to protect them.

ENTRY 2

06:02:15
The sixty-second burn took place right on schedule. I'm on my way to Mars. Honestly, I can't believe it...that I was chosen. Now all I can do is look back and watch the Earth disappear behind me. Believe me, it is hard to see, but this mission has to be done.

DAY 32

MAY 3, 2037

ENTRY 1

08:35:12

God, it is so lonely out here. Yeah, I get messages from Earth, but nothing else. I would love to have a call from Steph, but having a conversation is next to impossible because of the distance. I never realized how important Laurie and Steph are to me. They are so far away. No one has ever been this far away before. They surely don't know how to train you for this. Next week is Easter. I hope that Laurie gets something good. I brought a chocolate egg with me, so I can imagine that I'm here eating candy with her. I wonder...did Steph play that tape I made for Laurie? I know she won't understand, but it was more for me than it was for her. I close my eyes, and I can see her smile...I can see her smile.

DAY 33

May 4, 2037

ENTRY 1

20:56:38
I'm here at last. I'm the first human being to see

Mars this close. It is amazing. It really is. There are mountains and valleys, things that look like rivers flowing down from the polar areas. God, it is beautiful. I can see faint clouds, red clouds but clouds, none the less, floating across the surface. That was something that no one ever saw from Earth. I'm scheduled for ten orbits. I'm going to take as many pictures as I can before I leave. They are not going to believe this at home!

ENTRY 2

21:30:15

The rocket just fired, and I am finally out of Martian orbit. God, it was beautiful. I took more than 100 pictures. I cannot wait to show them to Steph. She is going to be so happy. I miss them so much; I have never been away from her for such a long time. I look out the front window, and I can see the Earth. It is just a small blue dot in space, but it is home. I can't wait to feel grass again. Yeah, I am suffering from major cabin fever, but I can't go outside to cure it, and the sun isn't giving me enough light to get rid of the feeling of loneliness. If I could hear her voice or see a picture of how much Laurie has changed it would help, but I don't think mission control is going to go for that. Damn it, I should have brought a picture with me, but we hadn't taken one yet. God, I am a freaking idiot. Oh well, thirty more days and I will be holding her again.

DAY 58

May 29, 2037

ENTRY 1

11:23:56

I am well on my way home. I heard something strange this morning. There was a loud bang that came from the back of the ship and I saw some metal fragments fly past the window. I don't know what it was, but the Earth is still in front of me. Radar says that I am traveling at more than 155,000 miles an hour. The way I figure it, I am still about 115 million kilometers from Earth. It is very possible that I should be home on time. I wonder if Laurie remembers me? It has been so long since I have seen her. I know that I am low on fuel. I'm not sure how much I have left. I hope it's enough to make it back home.... I can just hope. That is all I have left.

ENTRY 2

18:35:45

Whatever that sound was, it damaged the ship. I still have power and life support, but I have been knocked off course by ten degrees. With the distance I have yet to travel, I may miss Earth entirely. I will try some maneuvering thrusters to see if I can get back on course. A five minute burn should get me back on course. However, if it doesn't burn long enough, I will miss Earth, and if it burns too long, I will crash, most likely in the Pacific. I know one thing, it would not be good to strike the ocean at the speed I'm traveling. I have to do everything exactly just right.

ENTRY 3

19:21:00

Just received a message from Mission Control, they said that I was struck by a micro meteor that ruptured the skin of the ship. They also said their computers show that I have enough fuel for one try at correcting my course. After that, I'm at the mercy of space. I am so glad that I'm the only one on this mission. I could not stand myself if I was responsible for others on board. Yeah, I have been lonely, and I do miss my family, but if things don't work out, I'm the only one who will give up his life.

ENTRY 4

19:35:21

I just did the burn. I was going to run it for five minutes. That's what the computer said would correct my course. The burn only lasted for a minute and a half -- not near enough to make the correction. I'm going to try releasing oxygen through the vents. This might help me to turn the ship. I doubt that it will work, but I have to try.

ENTRY 5

20:01:45

It worked—just a little. Still a few degrees off course. I'm hoping that Mission Control can come up with something to correct this problem. The good news is that I still have enough air to make it home.

DAY 66

JUNE 6, 2035

ENTRY 1

08:27:00

I am getting more and more anxious. Mission Control hasn't come up with anything yet. They said that they may send a mission to rescue me, but I doubt that it would work. I'm going faster than anything they have sitting around. It is going to be so close. I can see the Earth coming toward my ship. It is so beautiful and blue. Even seeing the storms over the Atlantic is making my heart beat stronger. I want to go home. I want to kiss Steph, and I want to hold Laurie. Why did I volunteer to take this mission? I didn't land. I took pictures. A fucking robot could have done the same thing. What am I going to do?

ENTRY 2

12:45:15

I got a message today. Mission Control let me talk to Stephanie. It was only for five minutes, but for me, it was forever. I love her so much. How could this be happening to me? I just looked out the window. Earth is so close I could reach out and touch it...I could reach out and touch Steph.

DAY 67

JUNE 7, 2037

ENTRY 1

13:45:01

I am watching the Earth fly past me. The corrections didn't work that well. The computer's telling me that I am still 125,000 kilometers from Earth. The funny thing is, the Earth is on my right, and the moon is on my left and I can't land on either one of them. My family is so close, and I can't see them...I can't hold them. But I can love them and I always will.

ENTRY 2

18:51:42

I am going to shoot this record out through one of the vents. I hope that someone someday finds it, and if they do, I pray that they will make a copy and give it to Laurie to listen to when she gets old enough. Laurie, I love you and I always will. You were just a baby when I left, but please know that you will always be in my heart. Tell your mom that I love her. I just have one more thing to say before I open the hatch. This path will take me past the Earth and into the inner planets. I would rather die in the light of my home than on some deserted ball of rock. I miss my family, and I miss my planet. Goodbye to all. I am opening the hatch, so I have one second to say....

Tax Sale

Personally, I love going to sales—any kind of sale. My favorites, though, are garage sales, storage shed auctions and, best of all, tax sales. I have bought a few local properties that range in price from $500.00 for a small one-bedroom house to $8,790 for a three-bedroom house in one of the best parts of town.

In addition to getting properties at extremely low prices, when the previous owners leave, they pretty much always leave stuff behind. I have found hundreds of books, pieces of furniture and tons of money in these houses. My best find was over $30,000 in the attic of a house I paid $1,000 for. Pretty good day's earnings for just paying off taxes that somebody else couldn't afford. But, when I bought the house at 678 Spicer Street, I got more than anyone could ever imagine.

I searched the house right after I bought it. From the looks the inside, it had been empty for quite a few years. Everything was covered in a thick layer of gray dust. I mean, it was so thick—you couldn't see the real value of things. For example, there was an ebony dresser left in a bedroom. It had a beautiful dark brown and gold finish, but there was no way to see it until I took a heavy sponge and wiped it clean. When I first saw it, I swear to God that it was dull and worn. Yet that was an illusion created by the dust. Once I cleaned and polished it, I knew at that moment that I was looking at a sale price of almost $2,500.

The bedrooms were full of what they call "vintage" clothes. Every outfit in the closet came from the late 1970s. I'd never seen so many polyester suits. There were also bell bottom pants and a few gunny dresses. It was like taking a trip in a time machine back to an era when good fashion didn't matter.

On that first day I entered the house, after checking out the bedrooms on the second story, I walked back down to the first floor and then down the thirteen steps to the basement. I found so much stuff stored down there that it was mind boggling. The strange thing is, everything in the basement was antique medical equipment. Oh my God, I thought, this place looks like the shop Dr. Frankenstein had in that old horror film I saw when I was a kid. The walls were lined with old lead-covered bottles. It was hard to see, but I could tell that each bottle had a different body part inside. There were brains, lungs, hearts and everything else. Each bottle was marked M or F and then a date. Each one also designated what blood type the organ was. "What in the hell is this?" I asked out loud.

I knew that places like this were common back in the eighteenth and nineteenth centuries, but not in the last 150 years or so. I knew that, because of some documentaries I'd seen on the Discovery Channel. Doctors and not-quite-doctors set up operating rooms in their basements for people who didn't want to be seen in a hospital. God knows how many people were treated here and how many people died here.

I looked around a little bit more, especially at the jars that held the organs, and noticed there was a code of some kind written on them. The one with the brain had this written on a white, well-yellowed, paper: "Fe-MT3-22-46A." Okay, I figured the "Fe" meant female. The MT3 could mean the third Tuesday of March and that last piece—the 46—I could only guess at. But I thought it meant 1946. That had to be it. Every jar had a different code, but they were all in the same format.

In the corner of the basement room was a desk with a lamp on top. I reached over and switched on the lamp. It cast a strange light throughout the room…seriously strange. It was like the light you see in an old color photograph in your mom's photo album. It was a white light, but not quite white…more of an ivory. Yeah, it gave the area a really cool look, but I would not want to have to live with it.

The desk drawers were unlocked. I opened the bottom one on the left side and discovered it was full of small jars and vials — vials of blood-- I looked at them and found that each one was a vial of blood, each with the same codes as the jars with the organs. I quickly closed that drawer and opened another. Inside was a book. It was the "doctor's" note pad. I thumbed through it and found page after page of the codes listed there. I leafed through the pages until I found "Fe-MT3-22-46A." According to the notes, this organ was from a woman named Anna Louise Bailey. She was twenty-two years old, and she came in on March 19, 1946 for an abortion of twin girls. That was all the information that I could find about that patient in the book. After spending more time looking through the book it became obvious to me that the "doctor" had a massive business in abortions!

Taking the book with me, I went back

up to the living room, opened my laptop and ran a Google search for Anna Louise Bailey. I really wasn't expecting to find anything, so I was stunned to discover there were more than a thousand sites dedicated to this woman and what happened to her. I looked over a few of them, and they all told the same story: Miss Bailey disappeared on March 19th. There was an investigation, but the cased was closed after no trace of her could be found.

"Oh shit!" I yelled. My voice echoed through the room as clearly as if I was standing at the edge of the Grand Canyon. "What in the hell did I stumble into?" I wondered.

I sat there for a good forty five minutes or so taking in everything I had seen and read. What went on down in that basement? I was curious. I had to look around some more, so I went back downstairs. I ignored the jars and the desk. Now, I was interested in what was behind door number one. I walked slowly toward the closed door.

Did you ever get a feeling of total horror—the one you get when you are watching a really good horror film? Well, that was the way I felt, and it got stronger as I approached the door. By the time I reached for the doorknob, my body was shaking so bad that I could barely stand up.

The door opened slowly, held back by decades of rust and dirt. As I peered into the room, I could tell that there were no windows and no ventilation. The air was thick and heavy and smelled of mold and fungus. There was also no light, so I felt my way along the wall until I found a light switch. As soon as I turned it on, I saw what I kind of expected, but didn't really want to see. In my new house, there were bodies; a hundred bodies, at least—and they were all placed in different positions. The one closest to me was holding a rugby ball. He was placed in a running pose. Others were posed as ballet dancers, trapeze artists, soldiers and pin-up models. Every one of them had the skin completely removed. All I could see were their muscles, tendons and some of their bones.

Honestly, I had no idea that something like this could happen. But, for some reason, I was not shocked to see it. The bodies were strangely beautiful and very, very artistic. But I knew what I had to do. I took my cell phone and called 911. I wasn't quite sure how to report it or what to say. I just explained it the best way I could and, within minutes, the police, EMTs and the media showed up.

Then began the tedious job of matching

the DNA to their internal organs and to their skeletons I had found behind door number two. There was a third door, but I didn't open it, and I didn't want to be there when anyone else opened it. I may have been a coward, but after all that I had seen, I didn't want to see any more.

I walked up the stairs half sick; half frightened and laid down on the floor. My mind was swirling as they carried up one body after another. The bodies, once they were in the light, seemed almost natural … almost alive. The jars were brought out of the basement next and then the vials of blood. I couldn't watch. It was just way too disturbing. So I closed my eyes until everyone was gone.

A little more than seven months went by before I got a call from the authorities. They had found 135 bodies in the basement. Every one of them had died back in the early to mid-1940s, and every one of them had some kind of surgery done when they died on the table. Yet, not one of the families notified the police of a missing family member and there were no records of their deaths. Then they said something that shocked the hell out of me. Of the bodies they identified, all of them had grave sites at one of the local cemeteries. Right after that, they told me that all of the graves had coffins buried in them and every one of them had a department store mannequin inside.

"How many bodies did you identify?" I asked.

"Out of the 135 we found, we could only identify 131," the officer said. "The rest are at the morgue. We have no idea what to do with them."

I thought about this for a minute, and then I had an idea. I wasn't sure it was going to work, but I acted on it, anyway. I excused myself and went out and made a call on my cell. A few minutes later, I had my answer and it really felt like it would work.

"Well, what can I do for you?" the officer asked as soon as I walked into the police station a few hours later.

I explained my idea and asked permission to claim the final four bodies. He called someone—God knows who. A few minutes later, he came back and said that they were willing to do anything to get those bodies out of the morgue. Then he added that the lab techs down there were getting freaked out just knowing that they were there.

The next morning, I arrived at the

morgue. The bodies were waiting there for me. I loaded them into a truck and drove over to the local art museum. A few members of their staff unloaded them and then placed them in a sealed glass display area. This would be the first time ever that deceased human bodies would be used as sculptures. The exhibit is still on display for the public to admire so, never ever again, will these people be forgotten.

The Quilt Of Elsabeth Clarke-Worthington

There is a long history in America of people getting together to sew hundreds of small pieces of cloth together in order to create beautiful pieces of art. Quilts have been found going back to the first settlements on the North American continent. They were used for warmth, but even then, there was an artistic touch to them. Now, there are quilt shows and exhibits all around the world, and some of the pieces they present are worth thousands, if not millions, of dollars. However, there are still hundreds of thousands of quilts hiding in closets, attics and basements. This story is about one of those.

There once was a cabin just outside the city of James Fort, Virginia. It was not part of the settlement. For some reason, the person who built the cabin was chased from the colony immediately after the settlers made landfall. Whoever they were, they must have done something to offend everyone in the town because, for some reason, their name isn't listed among those who made the trip. It was ripped from the pages and possibly burned.

The cabin's stone foundation and some of their possessions were all that were found when a group of students discovered the site early in the twenty-first century. They did the right thing by reporting the site to the university, whose team did a complete archeological study there. They removed everything they could find, and also mapped the site as well as they could. But, once the archeological team left, the students returned and did their own expedition.

They did not stay at the site of the foundation. They knew that was picked clean, so they started searching farther and farther away. They did decide one thing. The students knew where the colony was set up, and they didn't think that there would be any way that whoever built that cabin would do anything back in that direction. The students also knew that most times, when someone built a cabin, they also built a second smaller building where they stored the things that were of no use in the main house.

The colony was to the east, so they started searching to the west of the site. Eileen Withrow, a senior at the university, seemed to be the one who took charge of the others. She led them into the forest and to a clearing about fifty yards from the home site. It was almost as if she had radar, because she led them to the far edge of the clearing where a large black rock sat on the grassless ground. "Dig here," she said. "Dig right next to that rock."

A couple of students began to dig. They dug down about three feet and then, when they didn't find anything, they started digging in a wider and wider circle. Eventually, they had a hole about fifteen feet across and three feet deep. "Go back to the center, and dig deeper," She said. "It is here. I know it's here somewhere, I would stake my life on it."

The students noted a sense of urgency in her voice, so they did as she said. They dug another three feet down and started spreading out when suddenly one of the shovels hit something. There was a sharp clanging sound.

It was very distinct—a sound they'd heard before when they dug in one of their backyards and found a really nice metal box filled with rings, necklaces and bracelets.

"There … keep digging there," Eileen yelled. "That has to be it." Everyone who wasn't digging, stared down into the hole.

The first thing they hit was a small iron pot. It was sealed with a lid, which was a surprise. They brought the pot to the surface. It took a couple of minutes to finish pulling it out. For being as old as it must have been, it was in surprisingly good condition. Someone pulled out a butter knife and pried the lid off. Pretty much everyone expected to see something—maybe some gold, hidden inside. But rather than gold, the pot was full of dried bones. "Hell," one of the girls said, "at least we got here in time for dinner." This made the group laugh and lightened the mood for pretty much everyone.

Two of the students jumped back into the hole and started digging deeper. After digging down about another two feet, they heard that clang sound again. This time they were more cautious with their excitement. They dug slowly around the edges of the object. It was a lot bigger than the pot they had found, and it was a rectangle rather than a circle.

As they dug, they realized it was big—really big. It took about an hour to dig this object up and there were a lot of inwardly guessing about what they had found. A number of the guesses involved treasure, but no one was actually willing to say anything for fear of putting a curse on the find.

The more they dug the more of the box they could see. It was a dark wood, possibly walnut. At one time, there must have been a luster to it, but age had dulled it. The wood was smooth and engraved with a cross that spread from one side of the box to the other. At each tip of the cross, there was a brilliant red stone. They could see silver handles and hinges. The box, even though still half buried, was showing its beauty and the excellent taste of the person who owned it.

"Get it up here," Eileen yelled. She wasn't 100 percent sure it was what she was looking for, but her heart was beating hard and her breaths were shorter and faster than normal. "I want to see what it is." Her voice was insistent, and also a bit scary, but the students did as she said and brought the chest up. They set it on the grass next to the hole.

"Open it," she said, as she walked over to it.

There was a big lock on the front. It was old and rusty, so it should have been easy to open. No one had a key. Hell, not one of them knew where to get a four hundred year old key. So one of the men walked over, grabbed a rock and smashed the lock into pieces. The whole chest shook as it was hit. Everyone was a little nervous about what they would find. A couple of the students removed the lock and started opening the lid. It moaned and creaked as they lifted it, but they did what they had to do to get it open. Once they lifted it up so far, it fell backward. The hinges were still strong, and they held the weight of the lid.

"What's in it?" a pretty girl standing toward the back asked. The same question echoed throughout the group as they all moved closer trying to see inside the chest. "Is there money?" she asked once again echoing what everyone else was thinking.

Eileen and a couple of the others walked over and looked carefully at what was in the box. First, they saw a leather pouch. It was black leather and had a little silver chain attached. Eileen opened it and found a piece of paper inside. It was aged and brittle, and it had writing on it that looked a lot like the quill writing they used in the Declaration of Independence. The ink was no longer black as it was when it was originally written. It was kind of a rusty brown. They knew that it was real, and it was old. There were enough TV shows that had old signatures being sold that they knew what to look for.

Eileen took the paper gently in her hands, and she started to read it, "To anyone who may find this may God bring all of his blessings upon you. I know that God is calling me, and I have less than a fortnight to finish my business. I was cast out for not believing in the Holy Mother. I do understand their feelings, although I do not understand their wisdom. I am leaving this chest for the daughter who was taken from me upon her birth. Please deliver this to her and have her complete the mission God has given me to perform. Other than that, I have no other requests. If you honor me by doing this small task I ask of you, then I shall be able to rest in Heaven in the arms of God." It was signed Elsabeth Clarke-Worthington.

Eileen folded the paper neatly and carefully placed back into the pouch as her face radiated with excitement. She planned to take it to the university after they found out more about the chest and everything that it contained. After replacing the note, the group looked inside again and saw that there was a wooden box that filled nearly half of the bottom of the chest. Two of the guys brought it up and set it down. This box was plain; it was walnut just like the chest, but it didn't have the silver pieces. Instead, it had simple wooden handles and nothing else on its surface.

It opened easily. There was no sound or hesitation with the hinges. It just fell open. Inside was a quilt, or maybe it would be better to say a half of a quilt. It was dark violet and black and the design was what one called in modern times, a log cabin. It was a very basic design by today's standards, but it did have a strange beauty to it. Lying beside it were strips of material. There were dozens of strips of linen with the same violet and black colors as the quilt. Along with all of that were homemade bone needles and the original thread that must have been used on the quilt when it was being sewn.

The rest of the chest was filled with clothes, several cooking tools and yes, there were some coins. They were shillings, and they were silver. They were also tarnished beyond belief, but they were still silver and possibly worth some money. A few had the face of King James I on them and then there were others that had a portrait of Queen Elizabeth I.

There were some interesting and possibly some valuable objects coming from the chest. Yet the only thing Eileen was interested in was the box with the quilt and the material in it. She felt some connection to it that she didn't understand, and she wouldn't have been able to explain it, if she did. As far as she was concerned, anything else, the others could split and do with it what they wanted.

Eileen grabbed the letter and the box that held the quilt, and she walked home. The others called to her, but she just kept going.

Once she got home, she read the letter again. There was something about it and about that box that intrigued her. She didn't know how to sew, so why in the world would she take a quilt? She always claimed that, when it came to art, she didn't know a t-square from piece of chalk. So why did she take what she took? She wasn't going to think about it right then. She was dirty and tired, so she put the box and the pouch under her bed, and soaked for a while in a nice long, hot bath. At last, she was ready for a good night's sleep.

The next morning, she woke up late.

There was no school, so she had the whole day free. The first thing she did, even before getting dressed, was to dig out the letter from Elsabeth Clarke-Worthington. She read it over and over again. Then she took the quilt out of the box and looked at it carefully. She looked at each stitch. She counted the stitches, and noticed how the swatches were pieced together. Then she studied the pattern and the material. She thought to herself, *how hard could it be*?

After getting dressed, she packed everything away, lifted the box and took it over to her grandmother's house. She knew that she couldn't sew by hand, but maybe with a machine, she just might be able to pull this off. "Grams," she said, "I have to borrow your sewing machine." Grams asked what Eileen was up to, and Eileen told her that she had a school project to finish before the following Monday. Grams agreed and gave Eileen some tips before she left for the day for a bingo tournament down at the church.

Eileen was now all alone with a quilt that was well over 400 years old, some pieces of cloth and not the faintest idea what to do next. She took two pieces of the material and placed them under the presser foot, the way her grandmother had shown her. She decided that the original thread may be too fragile to be used, so she loaded the machine with linen thread. The first few stitches went well. The material flowed beneath the presser foot just like a new piece she would have bought at Walmart.

Piece by piece, they went together, a lot easier and a lot faster that Eileen expected. The pattern seemed to make itself, as she kept sewing. It was so beautiful she couldn't take her eyes off of her work. By the time she was starting to feel hungry for lunch, she was down to the last few pieces. Still, eager to finish the project, she knew that she should eat something. So she went into her grandma's kitchen and made herself a cup of Ramen Noodles. It was all she needed, as she so wanted to hurry back and finish the work.

There were only ten pieces of material left in the box. By now she was skilled enough to sew those pieces in less than ten minutes. She stitched each one so carefully. There was no way she was going mess it up...not now. The last few stitches went into place. The corners were perfect. The seams were all ¼ inch just like that woman on TV said they should be.

After more than four centuries, Elsabeth

Clarke-Worthington's quilt was finally finished. Smiling, Eileen held it up in front of a mirror. "Elsabeth," she said, "I know you can't hear me. I know that I am not the daughter you wanted to fulfill your dream, but I am the next best thing!"

She started folding the quilt up to put it away when someone touched her on the shoulder. Eileen stood up and turned around. There was a woman standing just inches from her. She was dressed in period clothes. Although they were dirty, it was easy to see that she was of nobility.

"Young lady," the woman stated, "I do not know how to thank you. I have waited so long for that quilt to be completed, and now my wandering soul may finally be at rest. Please know that I will be watching you, protecting you, being the mother I wish I could have been to my own daughter. You are blessed my child." Then she just faded away.

The next day, Eileen took the quilt, the letter and the story over to the Jamestown museum. Once they heard the story of Elsabeth, and how she was run out of James Fort, they were more than interested in the quilt. They took it, restored the parts Elsabeth sewed, and it currently hangs in a museum in

Richmond where, Elsabeth Clarke-Worthington is now given the respect that she deserves.

An archeological project was started at the site of her cabin as well as the site where the quilt was uncovered. So far, they have found enough evidence to tell the entire truth about this woman, and the missing daughter whose great-great-great-great granddaughters are expected to attend a ceremony at Jamestown to make Elsabeth a citizen of the Jamestown colony—an honor too long overdue.

Uliana's Chamber

I was eleven when I got my first computer. I remember it was an old DOS machine. It wasn't the best one available. As a matter of fact, it wasn't even close. I think my dad bought it for me from some guy who was building them in his garage, but it worked well enough for me. I used to do all the usual stuff — play games, write up my school papers and chat with kids all over the world. Things were going just fine with me and this old computer until that day in 1991 when my life changed.

It was Christmas Eve, and I was in my room playing on the computer just trying to find someone—anyone—to talk to. I signed on as usual and went to this site—I don't remember the name now or even if it still exists. Anyway, I signed on and then waited for a couple hours after my bedtime. Yeah, my mom would come up and check to make sure I was asleep. Luckily, I had a key on my computer that would black out the screen even though it was still on. I could always hear Mom coming, and I would hit that key, and just climb under the blankets until she left...usually after a couple minutes of looking at me to make sure I wasn't faking it.

Now, I was lucky to have the computer, but we could not afford a camera to go with it. So for me, chat was without pictures.

I got back on the computer as soon as my mom left the room and there was someone sending a request to chat with me. Her screen name was littleblonde11. That sounded interesting, so I quickly accepted it, and when I did, there was a lot of static and white noise coming from my screen and speakers. In the midst of it all, I thought I saw the image of a young girl. She was cute, to say the least.

"Hello Randy, it is very nice to meet you," she said with a deep southern accent. Her picture was extremely hard to see. The snow was heavy, and the signal was broken up. I guess it was because of my dial-up connection but no matter what I was happy just to hear her voice.

We spent the entire night chatting. Her name was Lliana. She was eleven just like me with dark brown hair and light blue eyes. She also had the cutest freckles I had ever seen, and, being in the sixth grade, I saw quite a few of them, but hers were the best. While talking to her, I learnt that she had been taking the same classes I was, and she was good at geography just like I was. She was a single child and really wanted siblings. Unlike me, I had three sisters, and I didn't want them at all.

"Randy, I do have something to tell you," she said. I didn't know what it was, but it didn't sound like it was going to be good. "I have been sick since the day I was born. I spend my life in a room that is sealed off from the rest of the world. You are the first person I have talked to in more than four years." I could hear the tears in her voice as she continued, "The one thing I have always wanted for Christmas—the only thing I have ever wanted—is to just touch another person, and see them outside of this screen."

It was so sad what she was saying...so very sad that I just sat there crying my eyes out. I wanted to be with her just to talk or maybe play a game with her, but there was no way I could visit her in time for Christmas Day. I wanted to, believe me, I wanted to; but it just wasn't possible.

We were still talking when the sun began to come up and I told her that I had to get off line and get some sleep. She asked me what the sun looked like. I told her that it was bright orange behind some velvet clouds.

"That sounds so beautiful," she said. "I wish I could see it with you." I started to ask her if she had ever seen the sun but before I had the chance, she was gone.

I looked for her again on my computer screen every night for the next year. I thought I saw her a couple times, but it wasn't her. It happened to be another girl from across town who looked amazingly like her. Needless to say, I never spoke to her. I was looking for only one person, and that was Lliana but it was as if she had simply vanished.

Christmas Eve came around again, and, again, I was at the computer looking for Lliana. This time, after I had sat there through three hours of a hundred people wishing me Merry Christmas, the snow and static started again and I saw Lliana smiling at me. Her picture was grainy—worse than it was the year before but it didn't matter I was happy that I was still able to see her, even if it was difficult. She was just the same as she was the year before.

We talked all throughout the night. As the sun began to rise, I noticed that she looked tired. I really did not want her to leave, but knew it was time to say farewell. We both turned off our computers at the same time, but she stayed in my mind and dreams.

That went on for years, but the video was getting worse and worse until I could no longer see her. I could still hear her voice and at least that kept me happy.

The last time I talked to her was Christmas 2011. It had been twenty years, and we had never met except through the computer. Her voice was weak, and I had the feeling that was going to be the last time I would be able to talk to her, so I asked for her address. She was reluctant to give it to me, but by the time we signed out, she had told me where she lived, and I immediately started making plans to go see her.

"Please don't be shocked at what you see when we meet," she said before we signed out. "I am not what you are expecting."

"Lliana, I am sure that you are as beautiful as you were when we first started talking," I said.

By now, my feelings had grown for her. I didn't just look forward to talking to her, I based my whole life on those few hours we talked every year. My thoughts had turned to her alone. It was like I was obsessed with a woman I had never met. How could that be? In my mind, it was perfectly normal; but to others probably it was strange. I went to the airport, got a flight to Tallahassee and soon I was on my way.

I arrived at about 9 in the morning. The sun was shining as bright as could be. I thought that it was going to be a nice day. I left the terminal, flagged down a cab, gave him the address, and we started out. We drove out of town and headed down some back road. It was about forty-five minutes before we reached the address. I looked over and saw a glass building with one entrance and a chain link fence surrounding the whole property.

"What is this place?" I asked.

"It's a hospital for people who cannot be cured," the cab driver responded. "Most of the people who go in never come out."

So many thoughts ran through my head. Was Lliana dying? What could she possibly have that would put her in a place like that? Is she still alive?

The cab moved slowly through the gate. There were guards and they looked at us carefully, but didn't stop us. It was a long driveway, but we finally made it to the entrance of the building. As soon as I got out of the cab, a nurse was there to escort me inside.

"Welcome to the Angels Hospital of Mercy," she said with a smile.

I thanked her. As we walked, she took time to tell me about the work of the hospital and I told her about my yearly conversations with Lliana. Lliana must have been a favorite at the hospital because she started telling how she was a sweet girl who never gave them any trouble. She walked me down past ward after ward. The doors were all closed and locked, so I couldn't see what was inside, but I did notice that there was a security guard outside of each door.

We walked by door after door. They all looked the same until we got to one that had a sign on the front. "Ward 73" it said. This door had a guard too but the nurse just walked up to him and said a couple words before he opened the door and let us in. On the inside were a number of cryogenic tubes. Some were blue, and others were pink. I counted them on each side of the hallway and I was shocked. There were more than 100 chambers on each side.

"What are these?" I asked.

"They are where we keep our patients in the hope that one day we will find a cure for whatever illnesses they have," she said.

"You mean...,"

"No, they are all alive, just sleeping. This way they can survive for extended periods as long as we keep them in their chamber." Then she asked the question I was hoping she would. "Would you like to meet Lliana?"

I paused for a moment before I said that was what I had traveled so many miles to do. I got a little excited as we walked down the hallway. It was so cold in there that, by the time we made it down to Lliana, I was shivering and holding my arms tight to my chest in an effort to keep warm. Finally, we stopped, and I was looking at Lliana's face. It had not changed a bit since the first time I talked to her. She was still that cute little girl I had met so long ago. I just stood there and looked at her. She had the slightest smile on her face. I guessed that she was smiling because I said that I was coming, and she was frozen like that.

The nurse asked me again if I was sure I wanted to meet Lliana, and I said yes I did. I was not going to lie to a little girl. It was then that I noticed a small counter on the front of the door. It read 000001. I wondered what that was for. I turned and, as soon as I saw that the nurse was on a radio telling someone somewhere to open 73-37. With that, I heard a set of clicks and the door swung open.

I called her name and her eyes opened, and her smile got bigger. "Yes, I am Lliana," she said. "Are you Randy, the boy I have been talking to?" I nodded my head yes as the nurse helped her out of her chamber. "Randy, you are so much older than I imagined."

"Lliana," I laughed, "you are much younger than I thought you would be." I started toward her, and she backed away. I reached out to her and said, "Darling, I just want to give you a hug." With that, she walked toward me, and we hugged. It was so glorious!

"Is that a hug?" she asked. I said that it WAS a hug and that people greeted people they like with a hug.

"You like me?" she asked.

"Lliana, I have talked to you for so long. I needed to meet you and hug you," I said as I held her close. She tightened her hug so much I was nearly choking. "Yes, Lliana, I do like you...I like you a lot."

"I am happy," she said, with the biggest smile I had ever seen. We spent the next several hours just sitting together, hugging a lot and talking about her and her dreams and wishes. But all too soon, it was over. I walked back with her to her chamber. Before we arrived, she said, "May I ask one more question?"

"Sure," I said. My voice was cracking but I made sure not to show what I was feeling.

"Is today Christmas Eve?"

"Yes Lliana, today is Christmas Eve," I lied. It was really the 10th of January, but I was going to make that day Christmas Eve and let her be a little happy.

Lliana started to cry. "This is the best Christmas present I have ever gotten," she said. Then, with a bit of a giggle between her tears, she said, "As a matter of fact, this is the only Christmas present, I have ever gotten!"

I couldn't help myself, I started crying like a baby. The last thing we said to each other before they closed the door was,"I love you." Then the door closed and the counter dropped to 000000, and the lights in her chamber went dark.

The nurse's head lowered, and she began to cry. She didn't have to say a word, but after a minute she explained that Lliana was only allowed so many days out of her chamber, and those few hours with me were her last day. I broke down, slamming my hands on the chamber in a vain effort to wake her up. She looked so angelic, peaceful and happy. I was hoping that she would come back, but, at the same time, I was hoping she wouldn't.

There was no one to claim the body. Her family had given up on her decades before. So I claimed her and buried her right next to my mother in our family plot. I was the only person at her funeral, but that didn't matter. At the very least, she knew that she was loved before she died.

Years later I got married and we had a baby girl. My wife insisted on the name Stephanie, but I was more vocal and finally she was named Lliana. I never told my wife where I got the name, but as our daughter grew she so resembled that girl with dark brown hair, light blue eyes and the cutest freckles Lliana lived on, and she lived a happy life. I made sure of that.

The Lost Tunnel of Niagara

There is a story more than a thousand years old. It involves a secret Native American treasure worth more than a hundred million dollars in today's money. The thing is, no one has heard about it. It was spirited off by a Native American chief, and there was only one written record of it. That was on a stone buried on the Canadian side of the Niagara River. The thing is, that the record is written in a language that died out more than a thousand years ago.

A couple of years ago, an old man was walking around the whirlpool a few miles downriver from the falls. He was looking for strange stones at the bottom of the gorge. Now, he had been lucky most of the times he had been there before, but on this day the gods seemed were not shining down on him. Despite all of his searching, he had come up with absolutely nothing. Suddenly that changed, when he saw a stone sticking out of the rock wall. As soon as he pulled it out, he saw that it was cut into a rectangle and there was writing on it—actually two styles of writing, neither of which he could read. After he dug it out and, thinking that it might be worth something, he took it straight to the Niagara Falls Historical Society.

This was the first time he had taken anything there, so he did not know what kind of reaction he would get when he walked in carrying the stone. To his surprise, the reception he received was a hell of a lot better than he ever expected.

"Hello or bonjour," the man behind the counter said as he extended his hand in friendship. The old man told him that he spoke English. "Thank you very much, sir. How may I help you?"

The old man held out the stone tablet and said that he had found it down by the Whirlpool Rapids. "I collect rocks down there, and this was sticking out of the ground. It looks as if it has some kind of writing on it."

The man behind the counter took the rock, looked at it carefully, then gave it back to the old man and disappeared into a hallway leading to a series of rooms. The man ducked into the third room and, almost as soon as he went in, he and another man rushed back out and came hurrying into the lobby. "I am Dr. Fredric Depau, Director of the historical society. My assistant tells me that you have something that I should see."

"I found this down in the gorge," the old man said. "It was sticking out of the wall, I just had to do a little digging, and it came right out." He held the tablet out for the man to see. Depau took it gently and looked at it. It did have two kinds of writing on it just as the old man had thought. One was a Seneca Indian language that was used when the white men discovered the Niagara region, so it was easily readable. The other was older—much older...possibly more than a thousand years old.

Depau looked at it for several minutes, analyzing it in his mind. He knew that he had seen the writing before, but he had no idea what it said. "Oh my God," Depau said as he slowly sank into a chair. "Do you know what you have here?"

"I have no idea," the old man replied.

"Man, you have found a holy grail, the Rosetta Stone," Depau said while grasping the stone as hard as he could. "We can know what people have wanted to know ever since the first white man's eyes set foot on the falls."

"What does that mean?" the old man asked.

"My friend, you have found the key to a legend that has been told for a thousand years," he said, as his eyes darted back and forth between the texts. "This will answer a lot of questions."

"What questions?" the old man asked.

"There was an animal skin scroll written more than a thousand years ago. It was found up by the falls, but it was in a language that no one knew how to read. If I am right, by using this, we may be able to figure out what that scroll has to say. If I am right, you are going to be a very wealthy man. I can promise you that!"

After making a Xerox copy of the stone for the old man, he had him write down his name, address and phone number. "I should be calling you in a couple of weeks to let you know what we found out." The old man nodded in agreement, put the paper in his pocket and left for home.

For the next several weeks, Depau looked and relooked, read and reread the text, and finally, he was able to make a somewhat accurate translation of the ancient scroll. It read, "Under the falling water lies a tunnel. If you enter, you will walk a long way into the stones. There, I placed my treasure... a treasure meant for my people after I have left this world." The message was vague, but at least there was a glimmer of hope that maybe, just maybe, the treasure was still there.

"Holy shit," Depau yelled in a very non-academic tone. "We found it! We know where it is!" Immediately afterwards, rather after he calmed down enough, he was on the phone to set up a meeting at the University of Quebec. The meeting would involve himself, academics from the university and the leaders of the Seneca Nation.

The meeting lasted about seven hours. When it was done, there was a unanimous vote that an expedition would be launched to explore behind the falls and find out if, as they believed, there was a cave hiding treasure or if the entire thing was just a prank played several centuries earlier. The expedition was scheduled for the following week. It was to include Depau and five other scientists of different fields.

Finally, the day came. Their first stop

was to be at Table Rock where they all met and bowed their heads and said a prayer to The Lady of the Mist. They asked for her protection during their upcoming endeavor. Each tossed a silver dollar into the flowing water as a kind of blessing to the woman who was to protect them.

One by one, they entered the elevator which would take them down below the falls. It took about three minutes to make the trip to the bottom. Donning raincoats, they stepped out on the deck and, as they looked up, they finally saw the power that they were facing. There were more than 500,000 gallons flowing over the top of them.

"Oh my God," Depau said loud enough to be heard over the roar of the falls. "How in the hell are we supposed to get back in there?"

They all strained their eyes as they looked behind the falling water. There, hidden by the mist, was what could only be called the echo of a long unused footpath. It was badly beaten and covered with moss from side to side. And, from what they could view of it, it had large sections that were covered by rocks. Now, they were not the huge rocks that lay at the bottom of the American Falls, rather, they were small to medium in size. Not too bad, but they would make the trip challenging, to say the least.

Depau took the first step. The rock was slippery, but he managed to keep his balance. The others followed closely behind. Each slipped in the same spot, and yet they all still managed to keep their balance.

The roar of the water was deafening. They were caught between the water and the solid rock, so the sound was even louder than it was when they were standing up on Table Rock. The mist in the closed area was thick, so thick that, even with their raincoats on, within seconds, their clothes were soaked and their vision was cut down to just a couple of feet in front of them.

Step by step, they measured each movement they made. All of them knew one thing: If they slipped and fell into the raging water, there would be no chance to rescue them, and that meant sure death. Maybe they were showing bravery, maybe it was common sense, but they decided they didn't want ropes that tied them between each other. That way, if one fell the rest would not be pulled into the falls with them.

Their travel went slowly. Depau felt every inch of the rock wall with his hands as he moved along. There were hundreds of cracks in the otherwise solid wall. Even though he could not be heard, Depau asked, "How are we supposed to find the cave?"

His hand moved quickly over rock that had been beaten so long no wonder it was worn down to where the surface was smoother than a sheet of ice. Suddenly, he felt something that was more than a crack. They were about half way across the falls, and Depau's hand was touching something. He looked, smiled and yelled," It's here! I think we found it!" The word passed from one member to the next and, by the time it reached the end, all of them were all cheering.

There was a ledge outside of the hole he had found. It was just big enough for Depau and a couple of others to stand on. The rocks were moss-covered. They could see ferns growing between some of the small cracks that had been formed. The scientists noted that there was a slight wind blowing into the opening. But it wasn't, it was strong but not strong enough where they would have trouble maneuvering. They also noticed that it was a lot quieter than it had been for the last couple of hours.

Depau lead the group in. It was narrow,

but they were able to walk comfortably. Step by step they walked deeper and deeper into the tunnel. The light from the opening faded, and the flashlights came out. The light revealed a cave of such beauty that no one could believe what they were seeing. Pink quartz, blue azure and gem stones lined the walls. The floor was covered with wood planks, somewhat rotten, yes, but still able to hold a man's weight. The tunnel went on for more than a half a mile. By the time they reached the cavern, they were nearly exhausted.

"At last," Depau said as he entered the room. It looked like a cathedral. Stalactites hung from the ceiling. "This is so beautiful," he said.

He realized they were where they thought, according to the scroll, the treasure would be. The group spread out, and one of the scientists found a box, it was nearly rotted away, but the sides still held what remained of the lid. He handed to Depau who slowly lifted the lid and looked in. Inside was a single gold disk about the size of a quarter. That disk — that little piece of gold — proved that the legend was true.

After finding the one box, they searched and searched for several hours, but they found nothing else anywhere.

Yes, they were disappointed, but the expedition was thought of by each scientist as a glowing success. No, they didn't find the massive treasure they were looking for. But instead they had found the tunnel and the treasures that lined its walls and, in doing so, had proved an unknown part of history.

A week later Depau called the old man and told him that they did not find treasure they were looking for but they did find some gold and Depau did keep his word. He paid the man half of the gold coin's worth.

Shortly after that the Canadian and Ontario governments sealed the cave so that no one would or could go behind the falls to investigate it again. They even found a way to cover up the story so that very, very few people knew of the secret and they sworn not to say anything about it...ever.

As far as anyone knows, that old man still searches the walls of the Niagara escarpment. He has found a few artifacts, but nothing as important as the one he found that afternoon in the valley of the whirlpool.

Ghost Gold

The year was 1842. Indians still controlled much of the land in California, which was still eight years from becoming a state. Both Mexican and United States troops patrolled the mountains and countryside, except for one section of the territory. That was the area that was known as Valle De La Muerte or Death Valley.

Valle De La Muerte lived up to its name. Hundreds of settlers, both Mexican and American, lost their animals, their food, their hopes and finally their lives there. The floor of Valle De La Muerte was covered with the bodies of those who did not know where the sparse water holes were located.

One day, small group of American soldiers were ordered to patrol the edge of the desert. At midday they noticed a young Indian boy running into the valley. The boy was dressed as most Indians they had seen in the mountains, except for one thing. He wore bracelets that shone brighter than even the stars in the night skies.

The officer in change, Captain Fredrick George, ordered his troops to follow the young boy while making sure that they kept enough distance so as not to be seen or heard. They followed him for about an hour as he took pathways that no white man knew about. To the soldiers, it seemed like they had travelled an entire day.

Their horses were exhausted and almost dead from not having any water since they left their camp and the men were struggling to stay alive, as well. It was as if they had become the walking dead in the 130 degree heat of the valley.

Finally, the soldiers saw the boy walk into a small community of other Indians. Capt. George stopped a distance away and watched the natives from a ledge above the camp. He thought they seemed friendly, so he and his four men rode down to the village where they were invited to share a meal, a drink and a chance to rest in the shade.

As they rested, they watched as an Indian woman prepared something in a big, roughly-made metal pot. They were not sure what she was cooking. It didn't matter, they were hungry and would have eaten their horses if they weren't government property. As it turned out, they were served rattlesnake stew, but they didn't care. Food was food and that was that.

While they were eating, Capt. George noticed that all of the members of the tribe were wearing gold. It was not just a little gold. They wore more jewelry than he had ever seen…bracelets, necklaces, rings and headpieces all made of the precious metal.

After dinner, out of gratitude, Capt. George helped a young woman wash the dishes. As she scrubbed the grease from the cooking pot, he noticed that it was made of a shiny metal. "What in the hell?" he said as he looked closer. All of the pots and plates were made of the same gold as was the jewelry. Later on, after his Indian hosts had gone to sleep, he looked around the village and noted that the rocks surrounding the camp were all rose quartz, which was well known to be the rock all prospectors looked for—a rock that contains gold…usually a lot of gold.

Capt. George called his men together back on the ridge and showed them the gold pot. He also pointed out the rocks he had found. They whispered between themselves while the Indians happily went on sleeping down below. Not one of Capt. George's men said anything as they stared down at the Indian village.

"Father forgive us for what we have done, and what we are about to do," Capt. George said as he raised his eyes to face Heaven. He then flicked his finger, and the soldiers leveled their rifles. Within seconds, there was not an Indian man, woman or child, left alive in that village.

Capt. George ordered one of his men to get their horses, but it wasn't long before the soldier came back and reported that all of the horses were gone. "That's impossible," Capt. George said. But the soldier confirmed that, indeed, they were gone. "Did anyone leave the camp while we were eating?" he asked.

Another one of the soldiers answered, firmly stating that no one, Indian or soldier, left the camp while they were there.

"What in the hell..." their leader yelled. He then gave the order for the soldiers to climb down off of the rocks and pillage the village. The soldiers took every piece of gold from every dead body and stuffed it into their packs Capt. George picked up the large gold pot and didn't even bother putting it in his pack. He carried it with him, with the handle hung off the handle of his sword...like a grand trophy he had just won.

They now knew that they could not go

back to the fort. There would be too many questions that neither Capt. George nor his men wanted to answer. The nearest town was over thirty miles away. Not too far, except they would have to cross the desert during the hottest part of the day. Eager to leave the area, the men started out heading south.

They commenced the journey with a limited supply of water and overloaded packs, so the going was slow. They were less than a half mile away from the Indian village when the first soldier dropped. The men ran back to the man and saw a bullet hole in the back of his head. Not one of them heard a gunshot, nor did they see anyone when they looked around. The soldier had been shot, but there was no way for the man to be shot. It was just impossible.

Those remaining split the gold the dead man had been carrying. Yes, it increased the weight that each man was carrying, but gold was gold, and nothing was going to be left behind. Once the gold was packed, "Come on," Capt. George ordered. So the men left the body to the vultures, and continued walking. Soon, all that would be left behind would be bleached bones.

A mile and then another mile passed.

The men were hungry, thirsty and tired, but they knew that they had to make it to the town before they could rest because there was nothing around except desert, flat ground and heat. There was no chance for shade or water, so there was no reason to stop.

They had gone another half mile or so when another soldier dropped. Again there was no sound and no one around to fire a gun, but this time, the men saw what had happened. The private's chest exploded right in front of them. They had seen this kind of wound before and, when they turned the body over to examine it, their suspicions were confirmed. The young man was shot in the back by what looked like a bullet from a military rifle. They checked, yes they all had their weapons, including the one they had taken from the first dead soldier.

One of the terrified remaining two soldiers asked, "Captain, what's going on?"

"I don't know," Capt. George said. He was not just nervous, he was scared—more scared than any man should ever be but he could not show it. He was an officer, and he had to exhibit confidence to the men he had left. "Leave his gold. We have to keep going," he said as he started walking again, closely followed by the two men.

It took seven hours for them to cover the next five miles. By now, as they looked around they could still see the mountains surrounding the Indian village as well as the town in front of them in the far distance, but they knew that they were still miles and miles away so they just kept walking.

Capt. George continued to think about what had happened earlier in the day. His men were killed, yet there was no noise when those men fell, no gunshot, no sound of a bullet and the men ...they didn't scream. The thoughts shook him, but he just kept walking.

An hour later, Capt. George looked back and saw that he was alone. No one was in sight—his last soldiers had dropped, but he didn't know when or where.

There are no records written that explain what happened, but a few years, later the body of Captain Fredrick George was found about fifteen miles away from that small town. His body was merely bones, but it was easy to see that he had been shot in the back. When they looked at the body, they noticed one thing: his hand was still tightly gripping that golden pot. Thus began the legend of the Ghost Gold of Death Valley.

Since that time in 1842, the legend has grown, and dozens of people have searched for the Indian village. Some came back and expressed frustration while others might have found the gold because they simply never returned and were never heard of again. Yet people still come to town and still search for the gold and they always will.

aunt Victoria's Secret

So many times I was over at my Aunt Victoria's house. Sometimes it was just for a couple of hours and other times it was for a week or more. I always loved going there, and I let her know that on more than one occasion.

Now, my aunt was a stickler for cleanliness. I mean she would totally freak if we got the carpet dirty or dropped some food on the kitchen floor. But for that, she was the sweetest woman you could ever meet.

Her kids, my cousins, were a lot like me. We were normal kids with muddy faces, scraped knees and a couple of broken bones now and then, but she still loved us. Despite all the love she had for us, there were rules we had to follow. For instance, there was one room up on the third floor that, if we ever went near it, she would be more than happy to beat our asses with one of the willow boughs from the backyard.

I was almost twenty-five when she died. I cried for days before the job of cleaning out her house began. The first two floors were easy, and we did find some unexpected treasures like a statement for a certificate of deposit for nearly $100,000 as well as a room that housed a couple hundred dolls. Yeah, they were freaky, but we knew that she loved them more than life itself, so we donated them to a museum in New York City. She would be happy to know that the collection stayed together, that it was safe from harm and that thousands of kids each year would enjoy them.

The place had turned into an empty shell by the time we made it to that forbidden room. It was locked by one of the biggest padlocks I had ever seen. Luckily, Sara, my youngest cousin, eventually found the key in a large ebony chest my aunt kept in her bedroom. Even now, after more than twenty years, Sara had been afraid to open that chest. I think it's because we nicknamed it "The Coffin." Mainly that was because of how it looked, but who knows, it could have been a coffin in a previous life.

As we stood outside the forbidden door,

Sara took the key from her pocket and held it out in front of her. "You know my mom is looking down at us right now," she said with a smile. She paused for a minute and asked who was going to break the sacred seal. After a few more minutes of debate, my other cousin Theresa said that she would take the chance.

None of us knew what the curse was that Aunt Victoria placed on that room, and on anyone who had the utter nerve to be so curious that they would break her one and only cardinal rule. Maybe she didn't put a curse on that room. But we weren't sure.... after all, Aunt Victoria was a strange old bird, and we believed she was capable of pretty much anything.

The key was loose in the lock. We could hear the grit from nonuse as the teeth slid across the tumblers. Actually, the lock opened rather easily for its age. As the last tumbler dropped into place, a cloud of dust fell from the door frame. The cloud was so thick that we were gasping for our next breaths. It was nearly impossible to see the door or anything else in the area for at least two minutes. Once the dust settled, we moved forward toward the door only to notice another cloud behind us. Our footprints became buried as soon as we made them.

I reached over toward the doorknob. I saw that it was once tinted gold, but most of that had been worn off. It was cold to the touch. I don't mean just cool as it should have been in the fifty degree air, but it was cold — really cold. As a matter of fact, my hand stung from the cold when I touched the smooth metal surface. The knob turned with just a little effort and the door swung open.

We looked in, and there was a resounding, "What's in there? What can you see?" from all three of us. It was almost musical, but there was no music. Our voices almost had the sound of the times when we were telling ghost stories when we were little kids.

There was no light, so Sara felt inside along the walls around the door and finally found an old gas light. She took her lighter, lit it, and then stepped into the room. She turned the handle on the lamp and the flame shot to the ceiling before it settled down to a flame about four inches high. The room's interior was lined with shelves. I counted ten shelves on two of the walls. On each shelf were a large number of containers. Some were made of silver, some gold and more than a few were made out of beautiful ornamental glass.

We walked in. The light from the lamp reflected back and forth across the room leaving rainbows of light highlighted the walls. It was almost beautiful.

Theresa began walking around in the room. She was usually clueless but, for the first time, she used her eyes and brain before she used her mouth. "Sara, Rob get over here and look at this." We walked over, and there was a plaque on one of the silver containers. It read, "Elizabeth Marie Stone – 1924 – 1969." The one next to it read, "Paula Lynne Hannover – 1995."

"That's my sister," I yelled. "She died at birth. I remember how broken up Mom was. I was thirteen, and I had to hold her up. She was hurt so bad."

Theresa and Sara looked at all of the containers on the shelves. Each and every one of them had a name, a date of birth and a death date. There were a few that lacked any information and their lids was sitting next to them. Sara walked over and reached inside the closest empty container. She let out a yell that sounded like she had found a snake, or more likely a spider, but instead of either, she brought out a letter.

I took it from her and looked at the front of it. It read, "From Victoria Ann Stone to my eldest daughter." I didn't open it, I just handed it to Theresa.

She took it and fumbled with it for a moment. "What do I do with this?" she asked in her normal confused state.

"Open it," Sara responded. Theresa opened the letter, and she handed it right over to Sara.

"What does it say?" I asked.

"To my eldest daughter," Sara started. "If you are reading this, I must have passed on. Please know that I love all my children and my nephew. I do have one thing I have to tell you. You are standing among the ashes of every female member of my family. It has been a tradition in our family to store the ashes since the early eighteenth century. It is my hope that you will take on the responsibilities of maintaining this tradition. Please use one of the empty containers for my ashes. With all my love to all, your mother Victoria."

The next day, Sara and I went to collect Aunt Victoria's ashes and we did as she wished. Her ashes were placed in the silver container where the note was found. Sara bought out Theresa's share in the house and, as part of the tradition, Sara hid the room key away in a safe place, although she did make regular visits to clean and dust the room.

Unhappily, Theresa was the next to go. She was cremated and placed in a container right beside her mother. That is how Sara kept Aunt Victoria's secret for generations to come.

The Last of the Ice Dragons

Thousands of years ago, mythical beasts such as minotaurs and centaurs, as well as Pegasus, walked the Earth and they became legends because of stories told time and time again throughout the centuries. The creatures were real. Yet, when they died out, they became not the history they should have become, they became myths and legends.

One creature, though, lasted through the centuries. Some say dragons can still be found in distant forests and mountains. Tales have been told of massive winged dragons breathing fire and terrorizing the people of Earth. Those tales have been told as recently as the fifteenth century.

The last surviving dragon was supposedly killed in the British Isles in 1487, when a knight found it sleeping on the shores of the Thames River outside of London. However, there remained one that no one outside of a small town in New Zealand knew about. It was known as the Ice Dragon.

When the Maori people first colonized the island, there was a population of dragons that measured into the hundreds. Green forest dragons lived in the woodlands, white ice dragons lived in the mountains and the blue air dragons called the air, sky and clouds their home—homes that the gods had granted to the dragons when the world was young and man was just a glimmer in the gods' eyes.

When the settlements of people began, there was a tenuous peace between the human and the dragons. The humans farmed and hunted animals, which were not the prey of the dragons, and the dragons lived the same as they had since the beginning of time. That was until one day when the humans and the dragons clashed.

A young warrior was out hunting when he spotted a deer grazing on the side of a mountain. It was a hard climb, but the warrior made it, and, with one throw of his stone spear, the deer fell to the ground. Then with a slash of his obsidian knife, he cut the deer's throat. As it took its last breath, a blue dragon flew up from the valley and landed next to the warrior and his deer. This particular breed of deer lived only in the mountains and was well known to be the food of the dragons.

The dragon rose into an aggressive stance, roaring loudly. The roar was loud enough for every dragon within a hundred miles to be put on alert. Its open wings measured nearly twenty meters from one end to the other, its eyes were mere slits, and its mouth was open wide showing a set of teeth that no other creature in the history of time had. Claws that were twice the size of a lions gripped into the soil and an armor pointed tail whipped wildly in the cool air.

The warrior kept working on the deer trying to pretend that he did not notice the monster standing before him, but the dragon roared again and tore deep gashes into the ground. Finally looking up, the man saw that the dragon was now standing over him. Things stood frozen for several minutes until the dragon made a move. It reached down with his fore claws and grabbed the deer, cutting it nearly in half as it lifted it into the air.

The warrior was not about to let this creature steal a deer that he killed, so he grabbed his knife and lunged forward, slashing into the dragon's abdomen. Greenish blood flowed onto the ground covering the rocks where the deer once laid and the dragon's head whipped wildly as the pain of the wound sunk in. Finally, it froze perfectly still. Then, slowly its head turned toward the young man, the dragon looked at him, and, as it did, his eyes grew from slits into dish-shaped orbs of fiery reds, oranges and yellows. The black pupils swelled so large that looking at it was like looking into a cavern. There was another roar. It was not the same as the first. It was deeper, more guttural—more menacing! The dragon's throat grew into a glowing red as the roar became louder. It was only a second later that white hot flames shot from the dragon's mouth. The warrior immediately turned to ash and then to smoke as he fell. The dragon gasped for another breath and collapsed next to the warrior as it used the last of its strength to defend a meal for its young. This was how the war between man and dragon began, and it lasted well over a millennium.

As weapons improved, it became easier for the humans to hunt and kill the dragons. Soon, it came to a point where adult dragons were not the only ones men hunted. They went into the dragons' dens searching out the hibernating males, but also the young and even the females who were ripe with eggs. Each and every one died a sadistic death—slowly bleeding to death, their parts cut off for food or medicine, or even for trade with other islands and the people on the mainland of China. It got to where a dragon's tooth or a small bottle of blood could make a man rich through the trade.

Of course, the dragons retaliated against the human's aggressions. Dragons that had never seen the towns, now flew in stealing cattle, sheep and even resorting to stealing young children as they played in their yards. Adults were never touched, but hundreds of children, some as young as newborn, were taken from every village on the island.

The war escalated year after year until the human's desires for the death of all dragons were so advanced that the dragons could no longer defend themselves. It came to the point where the skies and forests of the island were void of evidence that dragons ever existed.

After more than nine hundred years, a boy who was about six years old came running back to his parents with a remarkable story. He had been playing at the bottom of a nearby glacier when he looked toward the top of the mountain and saw a white dragon. He said that he thought at first it may have been an angel, but when he looked, and looked again, he saw the shape of the dragons he had heard legends of.

As word spread, the hatreds of ages before came back into light. Talk began of how the dragons had drawn first blood and how they hunted the children of the villages. It did not take much provocation to incite the men to decide to kill the creature.

The mountain was a day's walk from the village and the air near the top was thin and cold...cold enough that a glacier lasted there for a million years. But the men of the village were determined to kill the dragon and they dragged the boy with them so he could show them where to go.

It was a long, hard climb with near vertical ice as smooth as the surface of a mirror, and with crevasses so deep they seemed to reach the center of the Earth. It took two days to complete the climb, but finally they reached an ice cave which was protected by rocks lifted by ancient earthquakes and ice a thousand years old. Before the cave entrance were footprints both human and dragon. The dragon's foot prints were so large that one of them could easily hold the body of the young child. Upon seeing this, the men became very cautious and had second thoughts about entering the cave.

However, one man volunteered to be the first to go in. The cave was beyond cold, and the light was filtered into shades of sky blue. It would have been almost beautiful except for the fact that he was there to kill the last dragon. He walked for what felt to be miles before he turned the corner and found himself face to face with a large, white female dragon. She was barely breathing as she slept. He just stood and looked at the creature. Suddenly, he noticed movement. Under her massive wing was a newborn baby white dragon.

The man looked around the cavern and saw bones of animals and humans. He could tell by their clothes that they had died too many years ago to count. All were carrying crude weapons made of flint and granite and all were wearing fur wrappings. It was clear to him that these deaths were not from his village and they were of no matter to him.

"I can't do this," he said as he turned away from the sleeping creature.

"Thank you young man," the dragon

said as she opened her eyes and raised her head.

"Are you one of the dragons who killed our children?" he asked as he took a step forward.

"No, I only killed to defend me and my babies. There were so many men who wanted to end my life and the lives of my children. I am sure that human females are the same with their young…willing to kill to defend them."

"They are," he replied. Thinking for a moment he took a step forward and looked into the eyes of the baby dragon. "Can he fly yet?"

"Yes," she replied. "Dragons can fly the moment they are hatched."

The man thought for another moment before saying anything else. "There are mountains on a land north of here. They have animals and the ice that you need to live," he said. "I will leave you alone, but you and your child must flee when the sun sets in the west. Other men will come and not listen to you or what you say."

"I will defend my baby," she said as smoke wafted up from her nostrils. "I will do what I have to."

"Then leave and fly north," he said in a

stronger voice. "They have new ways to kill you and I do not want that to happen." As he finished that sentence, he turned and walked back toward the cave's entrance. Before reaching it, he heard a soft roar behind him, but it was not a roar of anger. It was a roar telling the baby that it was time to go.

The man walked out of the cave. Immediately he was surrounded by those who wanted to know where the dragon was. He looked and saw that the sun was setting and he said, "It is too dangerous to go in after the sun has set. Wait until morning and we will take the dragon when it sleeps." The men bought it, and they settled in for a night's sleep.

During the night, when the new moon was at its apex, a huge wind came from the cave and then, just as quickly as it came, it was gone, and everything returned to a quiet state without even a breeze.

The next morning, as soon as the sun rose, all of the men rushed into the cave and quickly entered the cavern. The bones were still there along with a pile of broken eggshells. The mother and baby had gone, and there was nothing to kill so the frustrated men left the cave and walked back to the village where stories of the fight with the vicious white dragon became legend.

Meanwhile the white dragon, her baby and countless other generations found a home deep within the mountain range of the north where they live in peace.

In The Time Of Eiddoel Obwydd

On every planet in every galaxy throughout the universe, there is a time when the people celebrate the midpoint in the coldest time of the year—the point when day and night are the same length, when the dark time fades away, and the light takes over. On Earth, that time is called Christmas or the winter solstice. On the planet of Aragonia, it is called the Crystal Night.

Aragonia has a population of exactly 3,983,725,406. Out of that number, 3,983,725,405 celebrate the holiday. As a matter of fact, it is the one day of the year that the Aragonians most look forward to. Starting at sunrise, parties, parades and any kind of celebration you can think of takes place. It is a day when all of the races and species on the planet play together until the sun sets. Then a bonfire is lit in every town, village and city on

Aragonia and they are kept burning until the sun rises once again. They are lit to honor the coming of longer days and life for the planet.

This is the story about that one person in Aragonia who did not like the Crystal Night. His name was Eiddoel Ohwydd. He was a seventy-five-year-old descendant of Aragonian royalty.

His father, Emperor Renfrew VII, was known as the most generous leader the planet had ever known. Every Crystal Night, Emperor Renfrew made sure that each family had a big meal and a supply of wood for the cold nights. His mother, Empress Crystyn, made warm clothes through the year to keep everyone warm from the bitter cold.

Unlike his parents, Eiddoel was a miser. Despite his station in life, he felt that the planet owed him anything and everything he wanted without a thought to anyone else. He never gave anyone a single piece of brass, nor would he ever buy anyone a meal—not even his own mother and father. He would laugh his head off at the suffering of anyone worse off than he was. To say that he was the opposite of his family was to be gracious. He was as rotten as a piece of meat that was left to spoil, and that's why his parents disowned him and left him destitute and living on the streets.

Despite the fact that he was living on the streets, it wasn't too long before he opened a small shop. No one knew what he sold exactly, but he always managed to have whatever his customers wanted or needed. The thing was, his prices for everything were at least twice what any other shop in the area charged, and he never ever allowed anyone to buy anything on credit, but he almost always had customers. He was especially busy in the time before Crystal Night. On the actual night, Eiddoel would keep his shop open, but his prices increased. Still he had customers. Eventually, he became one of the richest men in the town.

After closing time at his shop, he would wander the streets alone, mumbling and knocking little children to the ground as he passed. Then when he got home, he would order his servants to continue working throughout the night, while he went into his den and drank a full bottle of Darcasian rum. He would always pass out when the alcohol ran out.

On Crystal Night, Eiddoel did his usual ritual, but this time the rum hit him harder than usual. He was sitting in his chair watching his fish swim back and forth in their bowl, when the alcohol hit him. He slumped down and fell into a deep sleep. It was so deep of a sleep that his snoring could be heard more than a mile away. Suddenly, that night, he heard a voice in his room. Thinking it was one of his servants, he just waved it off, but the voice became louder and more insistent.

"Eiddoel," it yelled, "it is time that you come with me." He woke up and stared at a shapeless black figure who was standing near his fireplace. "It is time."

"Time for what?" Eiddoel asked.

"I have been watching you since you were a child and I do not like what you have turned into," the figure said as it reached out its hand. "You have a lesson to learn."

Eiddoel felt powerless for the first time in his life as he took the figure's hand and they walked together through a mirror at the other end of the room. When they emerged, what Eiddoel saw was completely unfamiliar. It was Aragonia, but it was different.

"Where are we?" he asked.

"Do not ask questions," the figure said in a very stern voice. "Just watch and think."

In front of them was a boy. Eiddoel

guessed that he was no more than fifteen years old. He watched as the boy, who was wearing a large red cloak, went from child to child giving them pieces of chocolates, hard candies and some small toys. The boy never said a word. He just continued to do what he was doing. As he did this, the faces of the younger children lit up with smiles wider than even the river that flowed just a block away. Eiddoel could see that all of the shops in the village were open, and some of the proprietors were handing out little tokens that the kids would grab and stash in their pockets before running into the darkness.

"See that boy?" the figure asked. "Do you know his name?"

"No," he replied. "Should I?"

"No one ever knew his name," the figure replied. "He did the same thing year after year. He never asked for a thank you and he never wanted fame. He just wanted the children to be happy for one day out of the year."

"So?" Eiddoel asked.

"Because of him, the holy day of Crystal Night was born. It was more than 1,000 years before you were ever a thought in your mother's dreams."

"What happened to him?" Eiddoel asked.

"He died after a long life. He was never a rich man, but every year throughout his life he made sure that each child knew what it was like to have a smile.

He lived, penniless for 373 seasons. In his will, he asked to be buried in an unmarked grave. That wish was granted. It was the least the town could do for him." He took Eiddoel by the hand. "Eiddoel, what were your Crystal Nights like? I know that you had more presents than you could handle, and you were like those children. You had a smile that would last for days. Now, come with me." The figure pulled Eiddoel to its side and they walked through another mirror.

They emerged into a world that Eiddoel knew all too well. Walking around were hundreds of children, most of them were crying and the others just looked catatonic.

"What is wrong with them?" Eiddoel asked.

"People like you destroyed the true meaning of Crystal Night," the figure said. "Everyone has lost the spirit of giving. You have made it so that profit has become more important than the happiness of even the youngest child."

Eiddoel stood there looking at the children. They looked so sad. "But profit is what keeps our society going," he said.

"Eiddoel, how could you look into their faces—into their eyes—and say that any amount of money that you have made or will make means anything compared to those helpless children?"

"Is this...?" Eiddoel started to ask.

"Yes, this is your Crystal Night," the creature said. "There is your house up on the hill. It is impossible to see the suffering of the people down here when you put yourself so high above them." Then it told Eiddoel to follow, and it led him to the gates of his factory. They looked through the gate, and they saw hundreds of people working hard at their jobs. "Don't you think that those people would rather be at home with their children, celebrating Crystal Night in the best way they can?"

"I have to keep the company running," Eiddoel said. "The town needs the income that I pay out."

"Come with me," the figure said in an extremely firm voice.

"Where are we going?" Eiddoel asked,

as they walked into a store and stepped into a mirror.

The trip was fast. When they stepped out, they were standing in the middle of a cemetery. In the distance was a fenced off area. Inside the fence were graves marked by simple wooden crosses. There were people there. Some of them were digging up the graves and piling the bodies onto a horse drawn cart. Others were placing newly dead bodies into the graves, when the bodies were removed. Surrounding the area were thousands of people—most of them crying and shouting out their goodbyes to their families and friends.

Why are we here?" Eiddoel asked as he started shaking. He thought that he was shivering because of the cold, but it was obviously summertime and the air was somewhere around eighty-six degrees so it couldn't have been that. Maybe it was nerves. *Yes*, he thought. *That's what it is.* It was nerves, and he could control that.

"Look at those people," the figure commanded. "They are the ones who give you the life that you have, and they cannot even gain rest from their poverty even in death." The figure grabbed Eiddoel's arm hard as he continued, "That is because of you Ohwydd. You have taken everything including their lives. Is it worth being the way that you are when so many have to suffer for it?" Then he swung Eiddoel around, and he was then watching a funeral ceremony. There was only a priest and the coffin. The priest was having trouble granting the soul eternal rest.

Eiddoel looked up at the tomb. It was as tall as a two-story home and as wide as it was tall. It was made of sparkling black granite, and the doors were lined with gold and red gemstones from a mine more than a thousand miles away. "Whose is this?" Eiddoel asked.

"Can't you tell?" the figure asked.

Eiddoel stood there for a moment and didn't say a word. Irritated, the figure grabbed Eiddoel and threw him to the edge of the grave. The casket was open out of tradition. It would be closed only after all of the right prayers were said. Eiddoel's eyes opened, and he realized he was looking into his own face.

"I'm dead?" Eiddoel asked. "That can't be me. I was alive when we left."

"Eiddoel, that was some time ago," the figure said. "You died three days ago, and this is your funeral and your tomb. Doesn't it please you?"

"No it doesn't," Eiddoel said. "Where are all my friends and my family? I know that my kids would be at my funeral. They loved me more than anyone else ever could."

"They are fighting over who gets your money," the figure said with a laugh. "All of them want everything they can get, just like their father. Look over there," he said pointing at the poor section of the cemetery. They have so many people who will miss them, and will love them, even after they have died. You get a priest and a tomb that is twice as large as their houses."

"Why?" Eiddoel asked

"Because you have lived a life of hurting those who depended on you," it said. "You deserve, what life has given you."

"How old was I?" he asked.

"You were 378 seasons when you died."

Eiddoel started crying. This was completely out of his nature, but he couldn't help it.

"You died of sloth, greed, envy and gluttony. But you do not have to." Then there was a flash of light and Eiddoel was back in his chair. He was drooling, and his neck was sore, but at least he was back at home.

He looked through his living room

window and could see the children of the town lined up against his company's gate. It was the night before Crystal Night, and he could see everything. They were all kissing and hugging their fathers and mothers through the metal bars. In the distance, he could see the cemetery with the mourners standing over the graves offering gifts and singing songs to their family members. Again, he cried.

The next morning, he closed the factory and walked down to the town square. There was three-feet of fresh snow on the ground. He told some of the people there to gather everyone up...that he wanted to talk to them. It took about an hour to get everyone together.

"I have been a tyrant," he started. "I have been killing this town and all of the people. Starting at this moment, I am giving the company to the people who work there. I will just keep a one percent ownership to have money to live on. Other than that, the money will go to the people. I will move into a small house in town. The house on the hill is going to the kids of the town so that they may have a decent school where they can learn and grow." He pointed toward the cemetery. "Those people who are buried in the poorer section of the cemetery, will be moved and given a decent, free funeral, and there will be no bodies ever removed from their graves, ever again."

The crowd was more than excited. You could hear the celebration throughout the entire town. Within a few minutes, Eiddoel Ohwydd went from the most hated man alive to the savior of not only the town, but the entire planet.

He thought back to that creature and everything he had been told. He did change his life, and the lives of everyone he could see. When he died eighty seasons later, he was buried in a plain grave with a small stone to mark its place. At his gravesite, he had 10,000 mourners. No one knew whether Eiddoel was happy or not, but he did good, and he was buried with a smile on his face and thousands of flowers in his casket. Eiddoel will be remembered.

The Mermaid of Lake Erie

Throughout my time as a child, I have spent hours and hours fishing in the Portage Lakes. Many times I brought up crappies, sunfish, maybe a keeper bass, even a few freshwater clams and crayfish. Now, that was when I was using a cheap rod and reel and a bobber to let me know if and when I hooked a fish.

Now that I am a "grown-up," I sometimes still fish in those familiar lakes. Today though, I have my own boat and I do a lot of fishing in the Great Lakes, especially the waters between Long Point in Canada and Presque Isle in the United States. The fish there are bigger, stronger, and they will put up a more powerful fight than any fish I ever caught in shallower waters.

I remember one trip. It was a week before summer officially arrived and it was cool—about fifty-five degrees I think, and I

139

decided that I would go out and get some fishing done before the summer tourists arrived, and there would be too many people fishing to get the giant fish I wanted to catch. I found that within a few days after the tourists arrived for the season, those monsters went into even deeper water and would hide until the season was over in October.

That morning, I got down to the marina sometime around 6 a.m. Just as I knew it would be, the marina was full of boats but, other than the attendant, I was the only person walking around. Anyway, I filled my boat with fuel and started out. I waved to the attendant as I pulled out into the lake. At the same time, I noticed something strange. There were hundreds of fish covering the rocks where the marina opened into the lake. I'm not talking about just the smaller fish, but there were some lake trout that I guessed were more than seven feet long. These were a rare sight in open water and it was highly unusual to see more than a dozen of them washed up on the land. I made a quick note on my computer about what I had seen and set out to my favorite spot twelve miles off the coast of Presque Isle.

About a mile out, I turned on my fish tracker and put my headset on so I could hear the returning signal. By doing that, I not only can see where the fish are, but I can also hear how big the schools are.

Time passed slowly, which isn't uncommon when you are alone on a boat far beyond the sight of land. I saw and heard the usual traffic, birds hitting the water to catch the smaller fish in the lake, a couple schools of muskies and a few solitary lake trout. It wasn't until I was out about five miles that I hit onto something that was interesting. There was a school of salmon about a half a mile off to my right. Quickly I changed course. It would take about twenty minutes to reach the school, so I set the auto-navigation and went and got me a sandwich and a cup of coffee

I was only gone for a minute or two, but when I got back, I saw that the salmon were long gone. Yes, I was disappointed, but I did what I knew I should do. I increased the sensitivity of the fish hunter and settled back to eat my sandwich. It was just a second later that the alarm went off. I sat straight up. The salmon were just a little bit off to the right. I readjusted my course and started after them.

The course took me into deeper water. I knew I was almost in Canadian waters, but I kept following.

I travelled about another mile before something happened. From somewhere down in the water, I could hear a high-pitched sound. I hadn't put my headphones back on yet because I was still drinking my coffee, but the signal was so strong that my fish finder turned totally black. I could hear it all clearly from the back of the bridge, and it was not just one call, there were several that I could pick out over the next few minutes.

I looked around and then called out on my radio. There were no ships within fifteen miles of where I was, but I saw that the sound was closer, much closer than that. It was coming from no more than fifty feet below me, and it wasn't moving, so I turned off my motors and sat perfectly quiet with my boat bobbing in the waves.

I just sat there listening to chirps and whistles for the next hour. I was by myself, so I started talking to myself. "I have heard those sounds before," I said. "They sound like whales or dolphins, but the lake is fresh water, there is no way they could live here." For a few minutes, I didn't know exactly what to do, but that changed rather quickly. I got my rod and reel, tied on a big steel hook and baited it with a large minnow. Then I dropped the line into the water.

The screen was all black, but I could still hear everything that was going on. It took forever for my bait to drop down the fifty feet. When it reached that depth, I stopped it, set the reel to a slight drag and sat back ready to catch…probably nothing.

Suddenly, I felt a huge tug on my line. It was so strong that I was deathly afraid that either my pole would snap in half or that I would be dragged off the boat and into the depths where I would drown.

At the same time the line tightened, there was a loud high-pitched sound coming over the headset followed by another and another. Some were faint, and others were stronger. I could tell that the first one was still below me. Whatever it was, seemed to be in pain and fighting hard on the line.

"Great," I said as I fought the line, slowly winding it in while giving whatever it was a chance to rest while still wearing itself out. I thought at the time that it had to be a lake monster or something like that.

I was reeling it in for hour, after hour. The day had long since turned into a brilliant starry night. The moon was full, so I had enough light to keep going and, somehow, that coffee I had drunk was still giving me more energy than I should have had.

Finally, there it was, the yellow tag I always placed on my leaders. Only six feet to go. It was so hard reeling in that last bit of line that my muscles were on fire, and my mind was wandering but I still knew what I had to do. I had to get this damn thing up and on my boat.

I felt the line tighten as I started seeing the hook just below the surface. One more jerk and I would have it. By now, it felt heavier than the biggest fish I had ever caught, and that one was a seventy-five pound catfish that I pulled out of Presque Isle Bay.

One hard jerk and I finally saw what I had been fighting with for so long. Its appearance was a shock. I could see hair and wide open blue eyes that were glazed over. The skin was a grey color, so naturally I assumed that I had hooked a body of someone who had died and drifted out into the depths. However, the skin was not decomposed in any way. It looked as smooth and healthy as mine. Still I thought it was dead.

I dragged it onto the boat. Yeah, it was extremely heavy. I guessed it was over one hundred pounds.

I knelt down next to it and placed my hand on its body. The skin was warm, a lot warmer than it should have been. Its hair flowed down between a pair of human-like breasts. I could not believe what I was looking at. Suddenly it opened its eyes. Its eyes were the bluest I had ever seen. The hook still hung from a hole in the creature's bottom lip, I could see a look of pain in its face, like I had never seen before in anything I had ever caught.

I reached over and slowly, gently I removed the hook. I watched its eyes, and I could see tears flowing down its cheeks. Even though there were tears in its eyes, I saw its mouth form a slight smile. I looked at it and thought to myself, *My God ... what have I done?*

It opened its mouth, and the sound that came out was soft; almost forgiving. Now the tears were flowing down my cheeks.

How could I have done this? How could I have hurt something with a soul of its own?

Again I looked into its eyes. They were so human that I could not believe it.

I knew that I'd just made the biggest catch in history. I knew that my name would be well known. I also knew that, alive or dead, the scientists were going to have a field day over what I had caught.

Now, I was never much for fame or fortune. I just liked going out and catching a couple fish for dinner; but this was so much different.

I lifted its head and whispered, "I am so sorry I hurt you. I do not know what I could do to make it up to you."

She looked at me and smiled. I knew, then, what I had to do. I lifted her from the deck and slowly, gently lowered her into the water. She did not swim away as I thought she would. She lowered her face into the water and let out a call. Within minutes, several mermaids appeared in the water surrounding my boat. They all looked at me and then into the heavens, and they let loose with a loud scream.

I'm not sure what it meant, but as quickly as they arrived they were all gone, and

I was left alone with my boat, the stars and moon and one hell of a story to tell.

I have not shared this story in more than twenty years, but I am willing to do it now since, well, I am the only one who knows the location and besides that I am just an old man making up fables…or am I?

The White Rose

Many thousands of years ago, before the Roman and Grecian Empires, a country named Agoria was a minor power in ancient Europe. It was not an empire as the later cultures would be. The peoples of this land were all consulted before the king or his cabinet made any decisions. The country was wealthy with buildings made of the purest white granite with gold and silver lining the windows. The granite was imported from quarries more than one thousand miles away.

No one there ever had to suffer or want for anything. Not one person was without a home and every citizen always had more food than they could possibly use. They had a large port on the modern Balearic Sea. From there, they established trade with cultures from as far away as Asia and the Americas.

In the center of the capital city, there was a monument, but it was not a memorial for any warrior since the Agorians never fought wars.

It was not a monument for any one king or queen. They had their memorials in the forest where the bodies of the leaders were given back to the goddess of nature who provided for all of the citizens. It was a monument built to protect a single plant—a rose plant which had lived for more than two hundred generations.

The king or queen of Agoria had one main duty; they would go before the rose bush every day at sunrise, escorted by a specially trained squad of gardeners. They would kneel to offer prayers as well as a healthy feeding of water and fish blood to keep the bush alive. If the rose bush died, the king or queen would be executed on the spot, as would all members of their family. Fortunately, no king or queen was ever executed because of the loss of the plant.

The leaves of this rose bush were as black as the darkest pitch with a slight edge of midnight blue. The flowers were also black—a velvety black that absorbed any light that came near. However, the flowers were the magical part of the plant. Although rare, sometimes a single white rose would sprout from the blackness. It was found that, whenever a white rose sprouted, the king or queen would die within weeks. Needless to say, the people and the royal family, especially their children, kept a close eye on the rose bush waiting for a white rose to appear.

Raynor, son of Trisda, was king when Agoria was in its prime. He had reigned for more than eighty years without a challenge or conflict to speak of...until the weather of Agoria changed for the worse. The warm, wet breezes that blew in from the sea, suddenly changed direction and blew in from the mountains of the north. The air cooled and dried to a point where the climate changes could not go unnoticed. This caused the crops, which had always been plentiful, to wilt on the ground; and the animals died in the pastures. Despite the weather change, the rose bush continued to produce hundreds of black roses, which were picked and given to the children of the country as gifts from the king.

"Why would the gods turn their backs on us?" Raynor asked of his priests in a weak cracking voice. "They have always been so good to my people." His voice was one of serious concern, as nothing like that had ever happened to his people in their entire history.

"The gods are not speaking to us, your highness," the chief priest replied. "They seem to have left with the breezes of the sea."

"Have I or have I not been a good king?" Raynor asked. "I have tried my best and that is all I can do."

"Sire, the gods are not angry with you," the priest said. "They are pleased with you and they have granted you a long and beneficial life, have they not?"

"That they have."

"The white rose has been held back for so long, perhaps the gods have more plans for you than you may know. After all, they are gods, and you are just a mortal man—a king, but still just a man."

The king knew that everything they had said was true. It had been a very, very long time since the white rose came. Raynor was only just six years old when the white rose last appeared, and he was getting tired, and maybe the gods knew it. Every day Raynor made the walk into the city to care for the roses, and every day he saw nothing but black roses covering the plant. So every day for the last four years, he sat on the stairs of the monument and he cried.

During his reign, Raynor had seen his children being born, he watched as they married and when they died. He had fathered twenty-one children from three wives, only six were still alive. He had sixty-plus grandchildren and more than a hundred great-grandchildren. Even with such a big family, he lived alone in a castle with no one but servants to care for him.

The drought came in his eighty-fourth year as king. He struggled as much as he could to solve the problem, but to no avail. His health was too bad to face a problem such as this. Gone were his strong arms and legs, his breath was short and painful, and his mind was wandering between his real life and his life in a world his mind created. There were so many times when he prayed for the gods to take him, and there were many times that his physicians told him the gods would be calling him, but he held on, fighting the gods, fighting his body and fighting his mind. It got to the point where he had men carry him down to the rose bush in a litter, so he could do the duty he was born to do. But after a time, even that got to be too much for the king.

"Why can't there be a white rose?" he asked "...just a single white rose." His eyes were nothing more than slits, and his breathing was so shallow it could hardly be felt. No one answered his question.

One day one of Raynor's guards walked

into the king's chamber. He was solemn, and he kept his voice just above a whisper. "Your highness," he said as the king opened his eyes ever so slightly, "your highness, there has been a white rose." This pleased the king so much that he managed a smile. Weak as it was, it was still a smile.

"Are you sure?" the king asked.

"Yes, your highness. The entire plant is covered with white roses. There is not a black one to be seen. I picked one and brought it to you so that you may see that I am telling the truth," he said as he held the white rose in his hand.

The king took the rose. He was barely able to wrap his fingers around it, but he held it and brought it up to his face. He smiled a smile bigger than he had in a very long time. "There are more of these?" Raynor asked happily. The guard said that the bush had hundreds of them just as beautiful and as pure a white as the gods themselves could ever create. Raynor smiled again and said, "The gods have blessed me. Please tell my people that I am now happy."

"Yes your highness, I will make sure everyone knows," the guard said.

Raynor lowered his head onto his pillow

and, still smiling, the king took his last breath. After so many years, Raynor was now at rest.

The guard stood in place, crying as Raynor's eyes glazed over. He reached across and closed the king's eyelids and straightened out his clothes. The king must always look his best. As soon as he finished, the Crown Princess walked in. "Is my grandfather gone?" she asked.

"Yes your grace," he replied.

She stood there quietly. Maybe she was trying to think of what to say. Maybe she was so awe struck that she was speechless, but that only lasted for a minute. "I was down at the monument today," she said. "I sat on the stairs for hours asking the gods to help my grandfather. I looked and looked, but I never saw a white rose."

"Would you like the truth your grace?" the guard asked shyly hoping she would say no. But, of course, that didn't happen. She wanted the truth and nothing else. "Your grace, I have seen his highness suffering year after year. His body was done, but he held on to fulfill an ancient philosophy. His highness was dead, but his mind would not allow it."

"I understand," she said.

"I went to the coast and took a boat to

the other side of the sea. There, I bought a single white rose. I knew that he would let go once he believed that the gods had granted him with permission to die."

The princess didn't say a word for quite a while. She was thinking. It was so much to absorb. Finally, she took the guard by the hand and told him to sit next to her. "Young man, you brave young man," she started, "I proclaim that the gods did give him the white rose. It took a god blessing for you to have the courage to take a chance as you did. I just have one thing to say: Thank you on behalf of my grandfather." Then she kissed him on the cheek and walked with him out of the room to get a physician to verify that the king had passed.

It was an orderly transition. The princess was made queen and the guard who she met the day the king died… He was made the new queen's personal bodyguard.

After Raynor's funeral, a miracle happened. The warm wet breezes returned from the sea, the drought ended, and the rose bush, that gave all black flowers for centuries, sprang forth after a few days and there was not one black flower among them. It continues to bloom until this day, and until this day there has never been a single rose that wasn't the purest virginal white. Experts in roses have heard the story, and, in the king's honor, they named the flowers The Raynor's White Princess.

The Wolf's Babe's Curse

If I had known what was going to happen on that beautiful, sunny day, I would have made sure that I wouldn't have gotten out of bed. I would have stayed there with my blanket pulled up over my head sleeping, and hiding, instead of making that trip into the park that morning. I was just fourteen at the time little did I know then, that the hike was going to be the one thing that changed my life.

I went to bed the night before—I think it was something like 8:00 p.m. when I finally dozed off, and I woke up at 7:43. It was a nice day. The sun was out. There were a few clouds in the sky, but none of them threatened any rain and you could just smell the pine trees upon the mountains west of town. I packed a couple of sandwiches and grabbed some a couple of cans of pop...Mountain Dew I believe. I also grabbed my cell phone and stuck it deep into my pocket. You know it is astounding how much less stuff a girl needs to go on a hike. Yet, my dad usually had his knapsack filled to overflowing.

I started out at 9:00 and walked down a marked trail—one of three in the park. It ended after a couple of miles, so I decided that I would just keep walking and see what I could find. You see, my mom disappeared shortly after I was born, and my father raised me as a tomboy. I was always rock climbing, fishing or just going off on my own like I was on that day.

Anyway, the path ended and I kept going. The trees were thick, and the bushes were covered with thorns, so my legs got all cut up within the first few yards, but there had to be something down the way that I had never seen before. Yeah, it hurt a little to walk, but I wasn't going to let that bother me. I wanted to walk and walk was what I was going to do.

Like I said before, the trees were thick, maybe even thicker than they were before. I couldn't see the sun to guesstimate what time it was, but I knew that I had been walking for hours, and I was getting nervous. I tried to turn around and go back, but I had made so many twists and turns, I had no idea which direction I had to go. The sandwiches had gone long ago, and I was down to my last can of pop. It was opened, and I had taken a couple swigs out of it. It sure did taste good

Suddenly, out of the corner of my eye, I noticed something. There was a huge bush of Wolf's Bane. I remembered something I had seen on TV saying that if you digest a little Wolf's Bane, it works as a tranquilizer. There was something else that they said, but I was in so much pain from the cuts and had walked so far that, for the life of me, I couldn't remember what it was. I carefully picked three leaves, rolled them in my hand and swallowed them one by one. As soon as I ate the last one, I felt so relaxed that I ate three more and three more after that. By the end of the hour, I had eaten more than fifty leaves, and I laid down hoping that I would get some sleep.

All through the night I was having a combination of strong nightmares and cramps that were so bad, I lay in the fetal position holding my stomach. I was so miserable that I prayed to God all night long to take me, but no matter how much I asked, God ignored my request and He let me live.

In the morning, I awoke with the sun. Reaching into my backpack, I found not only the half can of pop, which I gulped down, but also my cell phone. Of course, the first thing I did was open it and check the signal. I must have gone farther than I thought. There was not one bar showing, despite the fact that I had ¾ of a charge left so that was out.

I started walking. I guessed I was traveling east since I could see a few beams of sunlight breaking through the trees. The trees were just as thick as they were before, but the bushes thinned out so, at least, I wasn't getting cut anymore. That was one big blessing, and it made my walking a lot faster...until I came to that fence.

About three miles from where I was sleeping, someone had erected a fourteen-foot tall chain link fence in the middle of the woods. On the other side of the fence, I could see that all of the trees had been cut down and that someone had planted a field of large, strangely green plants. Every couple of yards, there were motion detectors, with something hooked up to them. I had seen them before, and they were packets of C4, shaped and aimed to force the explosion toward the next detector.

Suddenly I heard voices coming from inside the fence. They were speaking some kind of a strange version of Spanish that I could not understand. There were at least six distinct voices. I wanted to yell, maybe get some help, but I thought better of it. My father had told me about poachers who would kill anyone who approached their cabins and, going by the security I could see, this place had to be a lot worse than just where poachers hang out. So I turned north once again and started walking. The woods were filled with Wolf's Bane and Fiddlehead Ferns. There was a restaurant back home that served Fiddleheads chopped into their spaghetti. Needless to say, I grabbed some of them and stuffed them into my bag. I grabbed some more of the Wolf's Bane, too. It wasn't bad tasting, and it filled me up. I will admit it also made me feel really strange—almost as if it was leading me somewhere.

Finally, I saw a creek up ahead of me. It was small, blue, and **so** welcoming. I walked down and knelt on the shore. I sipped some of the water and discovered that it was as sweet as I imagined it. The problem was that there was a big animal just up the creek from me. I was pretty sure it was a bear, but, to me, it looked a lot bigger than any bear I had ever seen before. Suddenly, it turned on me but, strangely, I didn't feel any fear. I just crouched down on my hands and knees as I lowered myself as low as I could toward the ground. I have no idea why I did what I did, but suddenly I let loose with a loud growl, and my teeth were bared as if I were ready for battle. The bear made two more steps toward me and then it ran off into the woods. For a moment, I felt powerful—too powerful, for an eighty-five pound girl.

"What in the hell was that?" I asked myself as I raised up to a standing position. With the danger having passed, I went back to drinking the sweet, refreshing water...this time without any interference.

A funny thing occurred to me as I started walking again: I knew that I was miles away from home, but the farther I walked, the more I felt welcome and that I was finally going home.

Things got even stranger. As I walked further into the woods, suddenly, my clothes started irritating my skin. It got so bad that I felt like I was in the fires of hell with no way out. I found a grove of grape vines. It was too early in the season for any fruit, but grape vines have things like tentacles that, if chewed, will relieve any thirst. I grabbed a couple handfuls and hid them in my backpack.

I then slowly removed my clothes, tossed them away and continued my trip in just my bra and panties. It wasn't totally soothing, but it helped ease my discomfort.

I traveled another ten or eleven miles before I settled down for the night. I ate some of the Wolf's Bane and drifted off to sleep. Sometime during the night I was awakened by the sounds of animals moving through the woods very close by. I didn't move, I just laid there until they wandered off, and then I fell back to sleep.

In the morning, I woke up and found a dead boar laying next to me. It was torn apart, and the flowing blood indicated that the thing had been killed less than a couple of hours before. My eyes darted back and forth, scanning the entire forest around me. There was nothing to be seen...not even tracks.

I looked at the boar, and suddenly I was hungry—very, very hungry. The fresh meat was right there. It was so close I could smell its musky scent. Without thinking, I launched myself from the ground, and suddenly, my face was buried into a gash along the animal's shoulder. The meat tasted so good—the blood flowed down into my throat. The taste was salty, and the blood was so warm, unlike anything I had ever experienced before

When I finished eating, I looked up, my face was now covered with fresh blood and pieces of flesh. Before me, on the other side of the boar, there were two of the biggest dogs I had ever seen. They began circling around me. I looked into the face of the largest one and our eyes locked. Both of them were watching every move I was making.

I crouched down as close to the ground as I could, without lowering my head. I bared my teeth and a low, guttural growl came out of my mouth, but this time, unlike the bear, the dogs didn't back away. They just circled and circled and circled for what must have been about an hour.

Suddenly, they came close in and sat— one on each side of me. They weren't growling or showing any aggression. They just sat peacefully at my side. After a while, they stood and started walking deeper into the forest. I followed them; I don't know why. I just had a feeling that I had better follow them.

They led me a couple of miles and then the woods started to thin out. All the way, they kept looking back and growling. Maybe they were talking to each other. I wasn't certain, but it sure as hell made me nervous.

It was getting late and I was hungry again, so I took some of the Wolf's Bane out of my pocket and started chewing on it. Both dogs turned to face me. Their teeth were bared as they approached me. "What do you want?" I asked. The next thing I knew, one of the dogs stuck his nose into my pocket and took a piece of the herb for himself. And then the other dog reached in and ate what I had left. Then they turned away and started walking again. This time, one was in front of me and the other was behind me.

It was another hour before I saw a break in the trees. The sun was burning bright and, even from a distance, I could see people walking around ahead in a valley. There were also more dogs like those that had been leading me.

As I approached the edge of the village, a woman came out to meet me. She was about five feet nine inches tall, well built with long, brownish gray hair. The thing I quickly noticed was that she was totally naked. She didn't even have the modesty to wrap a cloth or something around her.

"Desiree," she said as she reached for me, "do you not remember me?"

"No," I said as I backed away. "Who are you?"

"You probably do not remember me but you all to me. I am your mother," she replied.

"I have waited so long for you to find out who you really are and make the trip to me."

"What do you mean, who I am?" I asked.

"You are not a normal girl Desiree," she said. "That is why you could eat the Wolf's Bane and not die. It brought you here." She took my hand and led me into the village.

"What does THAT mean...I am not a normal girl?" I asked.

She didn't answer. Instead, she knelt down in front of me and invited me to sit. As I did, I could see a change in her.

She growled and snapped like an animal and then I watched as her skin began turning gray and became covered with hair—not just any hair, this was the rough hair of an animal. Her fingers blended together into paws, and her back became arched.

"You're my mother?" I said with a bit of doubt, a bit of fear and a bit of excitement in my voice. She didn't answer, but I could see that she was changing back. It really didn't take long for the transformation to finish and, as soon as it did, she stood up and faced me.

"Darling," she said, "there are people who have a gene in them that usually lies dormant as it did with you. I have a question...how much Wolf's Bane did you eat?"

I told her that I had eaten some the day before.

"How much did you eat?" she insisted.

"I started out eating three leaves and then another and another," I said. "Honestly, I have no idea how much I ate, but it relaxed me and help me sleep."

"You must have eaten a lot," she said. "It was all the leaves that you ate that activated the gene. Legend says that Wolf's Bane harms us but that is not true at all. It is what matures us into what we were meant to be."

"What does that mean?"

"You have become one of us," she said with a smile.

"One of you?"

"Yes, one of us," she repeated. "That gene turns normal people into Lycans." I knew what that meant. "Look around! Everyone here is a Lycan. We decided to settle here so that no humans would ever be harmed. People think of us as werewolves who come out when the moon is full. That is not true; we are not monsters. We are simply human with a gene left over from the birth of mammals."

I looked around as she suggested. The village was more of a farm, it had gardens and pens full of cows, pigs, horses and goats. My mother noticed what I was seeing and told me that the village survives on the animals they raise. "We have been here for more than two hundred years and no human has ever been harmed. Even if they found their way here, we were polite and escorted them back to safety."

"I have never heard of a Lycan community before," I said.

"You are used to Hollywood Lycans," she said. "We would never allow any of that to happen here."

That made me relax a little, and I relaxed even more when I saw children and babies being taken care of, and taken care of well.

"You have a decision to make," she said. "You are a Lycan, and we would accept you here with open arms or you can go back to where your hunger cannot be contained."

I thought about it for a minute. The thoughts were of my friends, my father and my sister. What if I lost control and I hurt one of them? I could not face that, so I looked my mother in the eyes and told her that I would stay with her.

I have been here for nearly fifteen years now, married a young Lycan and have two children of my own. I have made the complete transformation, and I have learned how to control my life as a Lycan. In all those years I have never hurt any humans.

I know that my Human family missed me, and no doubt held searches to find me, but after some time, I am sure that someone signed a paper saying that I had wandered off on my own, and died in the park. The way my thoughts went...Let them think that I am dead. It is better for me to be thought of as dead rather than for me hurt, or kill, a single human being.

The Ultimate Beer Experience

There is a place just south of town. I love going there because they bring in beers from all over the world. Some of these beers have so much alcohol that the state would consider them whiskeys, but they are beer. I have gotten drunk on beers from Turkey, China and even a beer from Wales that would knock you out cold if you drank more than two of them within a twenty-four hour period.

One evening me and my friend Julio went out there to try a new beer that we heard they had just received. All we knew was that it was from Marrakesh, Morocco and that it was so much stronger than any other beer in the world and that we had to try it!

When we got to the bar, we asked to see that miracle beer. The bartender showed us a little bottle filled with a thick black liquid. We were in shock, especially when we found out that a six ounce bottle would cost us $15. Now, I thought that I had paid some high prices for beer— sometimes $25 for a thirty-two-ounce bottle when I was in Montreal, but never anywhere near that high in the states...until now.

Julio and I both ordered one, but before the bartender would give them to us, he handed us a liability waiver to sign. This was something neither Julio nor I had ever experienced before, but, of course, we both signed.

Now, we had done a lot of stupid things in our lives. Often times we missed death by a matter of millimeters or seconds. But hey, these are our lives. So we whipped out $60 and ordered two of the beers each.

I will tell you, the first drink nearly knocked me on my ass. It actually did Julio, and he took a good five minutes to get back up on the barstool. Man, that stuff had a kick to it.

We looked up to where the mirror was—why there is usually a mirror in bars, I'll never know. Right there taped to the mirror was a sign that said, "Only two Moroccan beers sold per person during any one day." That was a warning, but Julio and I took it as a challenge…just as we always did! Our wives, more than once, said that we were little boys in men's bodies. I guess they were right. We had to drink three of them damn drinks.

It took us a while, but we managed to finish those two beers and man, we had a buzz on you would not believe unless you experienced it! Yet, we weren't drunk enough not to figure out a plan to get a third bottle for each of us.

The plan was that Julio would go to the other end of the bar and pick a fight with the biggest guy he could find. When the bartender went down to break it up I would sneak behind the bar and get the beers. It pretty much worked as planned. I did get out of the place with the beers, but poor Julio got his ass royally kicked. He was so bad off that, when we met down the street a few minutes later, he was laughing and pouring blood out of his mouth from several teeth being knocked out. That didn't faze him, so we went back to my place to finish off those two last beers.

We sat down on the couch, and I reached over for the bottle opener that I always kept on a nearby table. They opened rather easily, and we didn't take small swigs this time, we just chugged down every drop we had.

From now on, I'm telling you what happened to me since Julio disappeared and was found down at the corner of Main and Fifth Streets naked, standing on a mail box and doing an Irish jig. To this day, we never did find his clothes.

I just laid back on the couch...at least I thought I did, but when I closed my eyes, I saw the most amazing place. It was brightly colored with multicolored trees, bright orange grass and birds that glowed and left a trail when they flew by.

I suddenly was walking down a path that took me past a small stream. Well, at least the water was the same color as in the real world. I looked down at my clothes and for some weird reason I was dressed as an Indian. I have no idea why. I'm of German/Welsh decent, and there has never been an Indian in my family ever. I was wearing a loincloth, a deerskin vest with brightly colored designs and a headband with just one feather. In my hand was a spear with a couple dozen scalps tied to it. As I peered into the water at my reflection, I could see that I was painted up, but it was not the Indian paint I had always seen on TV. Rather, this paint kinda looked like the kind the amusement park artists paint on a kid's face when they want to look like a cat.

"What in the Hell?" I asked even though I did not see anyone around to answer the question. "Where am I?" I yelled as I started moving down a path that seemed to glow a bright iridescent green. I looked around, and it occurred to me that this was a strange color since nothing else was green.

Then I noticed that, although I was walking down the path, I wasn't moving. The ground, the trees, the bushes and the grass were kinda flowing around me and past me, yet I was not going anywhere. Even any animals I scared up were running down the trail, but they were not actually moving, anywhere either. Believe me, I didn't think I was drunk anymore, even though I sure as hell wished I was.

Down the way, I saw what looked like a house. Maybe I could talk to the person who lived there, I thought, and ask them what was going on. It was a nice looking cottage, kind of like those I saw in *Lord Of The Rings*. It was huge for a cottage. I was thinking that, if they had an extra bedroom, I could crash there for the night. Then, a strange thing happened. The closer I walked toward towards the cottage, the smaller it got until it was no more than three inches tall. I figured there was someone home since I saw smoke coming out of the chimney. So I knelt down and used my pinky to knock on the door. I heard some scampering, and then the door opened.

"Who are you and what do you want?" a little man asked. He was holding a musket which I assumed was loaded. Now, I knew it wouldn't hurt me, but I was cautious just in case. He yelled again, "I asked who are you and what do you want?" I could see that he was getting pissed.

I gave him my name and explained that I had no idea what I wanted and that I didn't even know where I was. "All I know is that I was at home, and then I was here," I said. "Can you tell me where I am?"

"How in the hell would I know where you are?" he yelled as he started pointing the musket at me.

"But you are the first person I have seen since I got here," I said.

Well, you got here didn't you," he said but before I could answer, he continued. "I'm sure that you will find your way down the right path."

"Let me guess...follow the yellow brick road," I said sarcastically. He didn't laugh or even respond. He just turned and went back into his house. Again I asked out loud, "Where in the hell am I?" He shouted something from inside his house, but I couldn't make it out, so I just found the path again and started walking.

It wasn't far down the path when I noticed two men standing; blocking the road. I knew from their dress that they were Egyptian guards. "Halt," the bigger of the two said. "You must be judged."

"Judged?" I asked.

The smaller of the guards walked over to me and placed his hand on my chest. "Osirus told us that you would be coming," he said as he reached his hand into my chest and pulled my beating heart out from my body. He held it in the air.

I felt no pain, and I was still alive, but very confused. "What in the...?" I started to ask, but I then remembered that part of entering the underworld was that you had to pass several tests.

The larger of the two guards set a feather on a scale. He said, "If you have not lived with honor in your life, your heart will be too heavy for the scale." He took my heart from the other guard and placed it on the other side of the scale.

I don't know why, but I was scared. "What is going on?" I asked as the scale swung back and forth. "I am not dead. My heart is in my chest, I can feel it beating, and you are nothing but an illusion." By now I was screaming my head off, but the guards were not listening to me. They were watching the scale. "I do not want to be here." The scale stopped moving and, yes my heart was heavier than the feather. "That cannot be," I yelled. "I have never done anything wrong!"

They looked at the scalps attached to the spear I was carrying. "What about those?" one of them asked. "I'm sure that you had to kill someone to get those."

"I never killed anyone," I yelled. "You can ask anyone who knows me. I am a very peaceful person." By now the fear I was feeling had turned to pure panic. I had no idea what these two were going to do or what the punishment was for failing the test.

"You may not pass to the land of those who lived with honor," they said in unison. "You are condemned..."

"Here it goes," I said under by breath.

"...to continue on this path so that you may purify your soul and then return to us for judgment," he said without paying any attention to my mumblings. "You will have one more chance and then your soul will be vanquished to wander the void for all eternity." They parted and opened the path for me to continue but, before I left, they grabbed me and shoved my heart back into my chest. I thanked them—yes, I am a sarcastic ass—and once again started on my way.

I walked for about ten minutes before I looked at my chest, there was no pain, no wound and no blood. I wasn't far away, so I turned around and looked back, the soldiers were gone, and so was the part of the path I had just walked.

I still hadn't figured out what was going on. Was I dead? I hoped not, but I do have to say that if I was, this place had some possibilities. If only I could find someone who didn't want to kill me, or take my soul, but now there was a question that I couldn't answer or even take a guess at: what was coming next? "How much of this am I going to have to take?" I asked, knowing that I most likely was not going to get an answer.

"You have to prove yourself before you can relax," a voice said from behind me. "At the end of your journey, you will learn the truth of life that you must always keep with you."

I turned and saw, what I guessed was, an old man standing in front of me wearing a tattered robe with a golden collar and belt and no shoes. He looked like an old hippie I knew when I lived in San Francisco. "Who the hell are you?" I asked.

"You don't remember me?" he asked. He looked like I had really hurt his feelings. "You passed by my shop every day for nearly ten years. Every day I would give you a cup of special tea, but you never came in the store; we just talked on the street."

Oh my God, I thought. That *was* the old hippie. I knew he looked familiar, but I heard he had died years ago.

"Remember all those times I told you about the region between life and death?" he asked. I was shaking, but not enough to keep me from telling him that I remembered some of it, but I really never paid much attention to what he'd said. "This is one of those regions," he continued. "You will meet someone on this journey who will help you find the truth."

"That isn't you?" I asked.

"No, I am not the one. Just continue down this path and make the right decisions and he will appear," he said.

"One question please. Why am...I..." I started to ask, but he faded into nothingness before I could finish. It was then that I looked around again. All of the bright colors, the trees, the clouds and everything else were gone. Everything was the same as it was in my normal reality, except that it was dark, very dark; but I could still see everything.

I stood there for what seemed to be an hour when I looked up into a star-filled sky. As I watched, a large meteor shot across the sky. It was close and bright enough to turn night into day. I could see the tops of the trees sway in the breeze as the meteor passed by. I noticed that it was flying directly over the path I was traveling. A couple of seconds later, I saw a bright flash from just over the hill and then a blast wave hit me and sent me flying at least twenty feet back down the path I had just covered.

Suddenly, the entire area was burning, and the air was filled with a thick black smoke. I could see the heat in the air, but I could not feel it and, despite the smoke, I was still able to breathe easily. As I started down the trail again, the smoke parted for me and closed again once I passed. Yeah, it was strange, but whatever it was, strange seemed to be the norm, so I just accepted it.

When I got up to the top of the hill, I could see a burning crater on the other side. It was big, and the heat must have been incredible because most of the rocks, as well as the ground, were molten. It was bright red with yellow flames shooting into the sky, but the path wasn't affected. I stepped between the flames. The ground was bubbling around me, and I could feel the boiling just inches beneath my feet. I could smell the sulfur from the liquid, but it wasn't making me feel sick and I still had no trouble breathing.

I kept walking. Although it looked like hell—at least the hell that most preacher men talk about—for me, it was more like a walk in the town's square.

As I reached the crest of the crater, I was shocked to see that the inside of the crater was burning more fiercely than anywhere in the area. The flames were no longer the red/yellow I had walked through. They were blue/white was thick.

The path led into the crater, so I did what I was told. I followed it. I could not believe the damage inside there. I had been to a crater in Arizona but, despite the similarities, I could never visualize this type of damage ever happening on Earth.

I walked over the final ridge inside the crater and saw something I never expected to see—a cool spot in the middle of all that fire. There were trees, bushes and everything that had been destroyed when the meteor hit the ground, were all still there. I walked into the middle and looked around, it was normal—at least more normal than anything else I had seen or felt for the last two hours.

"Young man, drop your spear," a figure said as it, rather, he walked from the flames followed by two other men. They were dressed is robes that were beyond my ability to describe with the written word. Each of the men were wearing Indian war bonnets that were grander than anything any chief ever wore. Even the feathers which covered the bonnets were fantastic. They were every color in the spectrum, but brighter and more vibrant than any colors I had ever seen. It almost looked as if they were granted to those three men by the son of God himself.

I looked at the three men with a mixture of awe and confusion. "Where did you come from?" I asked.

"We have been with you from the second you were born," one of them explained.

"We are your guardian angels sent to protect you and guide you through your life."

I was even more confused than I was before. "But I am not an Indi...Native American," I said. "My blood is European."

"That does not matter," another of them told me. "All beings on the planet are children of Mother Earth and are all seen as equal by us. Humans are the same as the lowly slug that crawls through the gardens. Every one of them deserve and receive guidance and protection from us." I just nodded as he continued, "We have watched as you made mistakes in your life by not listening to us—that hidden voice in your head."

"Oh?" I responded in surprise.

"Yes, such as drinking something that you have no idea what it was made from," he said.

The beers, I thought. I thought back and remembered that I was told I could only drink two of the beers, but I took a third one. I knew I shouldn't do it, but I did. "I am sorry that I didn't listen to you," I said as humility flowed through my veins. Then, I lowered my head and asked the three men a question "Am I dead?" I realize it was blunt, but I had to know.

"No, you are not dead," one of them

said. "This was a warning to show you that your life is worth something and that the behavior you took part in does not show the respect that Mother Earth's creation deserves. We will be watching you from now on. When you see a hawk circling above, it will be us. When you see a sparrow looking for seeds, that will be us and when you see a cat sitting on a window sill that will be us. Remember what we have said on this day and you will be allowed to live a full life."

I swore right then and there that I would change. They must have believed me because there was a flash of light and I found myself awake and standing up. The problem was, I was naked in the middle of Times Square having my arms pulled behind me and handcuffs locked so I couldn't move. I was arrested for public nudity and fined $300. After what I went through in that crazy dream or hallucination...or whatever the hell it was, I happily paid the fine and was released.

Since that day, I have straightened my life out...well, somewhat. I still chase women, and I still drink beer, but now I never try anything I have never heard of. My main drink now is good old Coors and maybe a Jack and Coke once in a while, but no matter what, I remember what I was told—that I am being watched and protected by everything on Earth and that kept me going through the next fifty years.

Vyzen and the Vodou Queen

There are stores in every major city in America that sell wands, herbs and other items that can be used to cast spells either for good or bad purposes. Some of them even sell Vodou dolls and other paraphernalia that are used for the more exotic curses and potions of the Vodou religion. Still, if you really want the good stuff, you have to go to New Orleans. Shops there have the greatest collection of Vodou charms and potions outside of Africa or the Caribbean. One store just off of Bourbon Street has the best of the best, and the people there have the knowledge about how to use it.

There was a beautiful girl named Vanessa Hoover. She was twenty-three years old with black hair, black eyes and wore black clothes. Everyone knew her by the name Vyzen. She was raised a nice little Catholic girl who attended church every week and went to a Catholic school, but around the time she turned nineteen, she had become interested in Wicca. She joined a coven and turned away from the church. She eventually became bored with white magic and decided to break away and form a coven of witches who practiced the dark side.

Vyzen and her "friends" felt that they had learnt as much as they could about Vodou in Allegheny Heights, so they raised some money and took the 1,100 mile trip to New Orleans. They had heard of the Vodou royalty who lived there, and they wanted to study under them for as long as it took to gain true knowledge of their new craft.

Ironically, on October 31st, the Celtic holy day of Samhain, Vyzen's friends decided that would be a good day to go to the various Cities of the Dead located all over the city. Instead, Vyzen left them to visit the shop of the High Priestess of New Orleans, as she had something more she wanted to learn about black magic and spells from the High Priestess at the shop.

When she arrived at the shop, she discovered that the windows were sealed, and the door was swollen so badly that it took her a great deal of effort to open it and walk in. Inside, besides finding the store in disarray, there was something different about it— something that she had never noticed before. She didn't know what it was, but something was not in place.

"Your Highness," she called out. That would have been strange in any other place, but the owner was a High Priestess and considered to be royalty. Some, within the religion, even called her a queen. "Your Highness," she yelled, just before realizing what was different. All of the mirrors were covered with thick black cloths, and there was a lit candle in front of every one of them right beside a small vial of some dark green liquid.

Vyzen walked around the shop making sure not to touch anything. She had learned that everything in that store could either be a blessing or a curse, depending on so many factors, mainly the hidden being that lives deep within everything on the planet.

Again she yelled, but this time she heard a scraping noise coming from a room in the back of the store. No one was ever allowed back there. Vyzen wasn't sure if it was the High Priestess's alter room or maybe a place where she mixed her potions. All she did know was that nothing was normal that day. Despite the fact that the sound was coming from a forbidden room and she wanted to know what it was. +

As she walked toward the room, she noticed that there was a blue curtain hung over the door. It was a very dark blue, almost black, and it had a pagan star woven into the material and a gold trim that went all the way around it. She moved it and, while the light was coming in, she looked around the room and saw that there were hundreds of vials and almost as many books. Statues of dragons and demons lined the walls and, throughout the room, there were candles of many different colors. Vyzen knew that each color had a meaning, but, at that moment, she couldn't remember any of them. In the center of the room was a huge chair— its back facing the door. Vyzen could not see who, if anyone, was seated in it.

"Your Highness," Vyzen said in a voice that was almost a whisper.

"Yes child, I am here," the woman said.

Vyzen walked around to the front of the chair. Her eyes had become accustomed to the low light by then, and she was able to see everything. The Vodou Priestess was dressed in a black cloak and dress with a gold headband with feathers draped on either side of her face. On her lap was an animal skull. It looked like a bear, but Vyzen had no idea exactly what it was.

"Come here, child," the High Priestess said. She was calm...almost too calm. "I have something that I have to tell you." Vyzen moved closer and, for the first time, she saw what the High Priestess looked like. She had met her on more than one occasion when she was taking classes, but the woman always wore a thick veil so no one could ever see her face.

According to Vyzen she looked no more than sixty-five years old, despite the fact that she claimed to be more than 250. Yet, she had documents to prove it. "I have not taught you everything you need to know...not yet. However, I feel that it is time for you to prove yourself and your commitment."

"I will do as you ask, Your Highness," Vyzen replied with a smile.

"Do not smile," the woman commanded. "My shop was stolen from. This man took a Vodou doll and a potion. I need to get it back."

"A doll and a potion?" Vyzen asked.

"Yes," the Vodou Queen replied. "He is

using it against me to take my position in our religion." Then she turned her face and looked directly at Vyzen. The girl could see that she was bleeding from her eye sockets, and that her eyes were both gone. Just the empty bloody sockets remained.

"How?" Vyzen asked, as she tried to stay calm. Inside, she was recoiling in horror.

"That doll he stole," the Priestess stated, "he knows how to use it, and he is using it against me. I could feel the needle as it went through my eyes. I felt them as he ripped them out. It was the purest agony I have ever felt."

She gave Vyzen the name of the man and where she could find him, so that she could revenge what he has done to her. Vyzen started to leave. She now knew what she had to do, but, before she left, the old woman called out warning her to be careful. The High Priestess reminded her that Vodou was nothing to be taken for granted. Just before leaving the shop, Vyzen grabbed some potions and a Vodou doll.

As soon as she was outside, Vyzen called 911 to have someone come and take care of the High Priestess. Before she left for the City of the Dead she waited to hear the ambulance sirens coming toward the shop, but as soon as she heard them she took off running down Canal Street toward the cemetery.

It took her longer to get there than if she'd taken the street car, and she was nearly passing out by the time she reached her friends. But she made it. She was determined to live up to the responsibility the High Priestess had entrusted her with. When she arrived, there was a chorus of "Vyzen what's wrong?" She sat on the steps of one of the mausoleums and explained the entire story. "I want to check something before we go," she said. She knew one thing about this cemetery — and that was there was a legendary tomb of one of the first Vodou Queens in New Orleans and often people would put tributes in front of the doors. The walls and the doors were covered with the symbol XXX as a tribute to the dead queen. Vyzen had a hunch, and she had to check it out.

It was disturbing, but the thoughts that Vyzen had were true. When she reached the tomb, she discovered that the front of it was covered with playing cards, lottery tickets, dolls and pictures of those who had died, including pictures of newborn babies. There were even pictures of sonograms of unborn babies. Vyzen could also see that the pictures had been disturbed and that there was a box hidden under some of them. She wanted to see what was in that box.

"Grab me that box," Vyzen commanded one of her friends. It wasn't like her to be strict, especially with her coven, but that had changed. She knew what she wanted, and she was going to have it. Once she got the box in her hands, she opened it. Inside was a Vodou doll that looked as if it was new, except that it was covered with blood. She took the doll and held it up. It was then that she noticed a sterling silver needle shoved through both eyes. It was then that she knew that her feelings were right. This was the doll that was used to blind the High Priestess in the shop.

She tossed the box back to the girl who had picked it up. It really wasn't a good toss because the girl missed it and it fell to the ground, breaking into pieces as it hit the walkway. When it hit, a hidden compartment was revealed. Vyzen's friend examined the box further, and found a black bag, tied with a gold string, hiding in it.

"What in the hell is that?" Vyzen yelled as she dropped the doll and reached for the bag. She was so frantic to grab it that she nearly lost her footing and went head first into the steps of the tomb. When she did grab it, she felt that there was something inside. Deciding to open the bag later, she picked up the doll, and they all started back to the hotel.

Once safe inside their room, the group ordered some dinner and sat down with some wine. Unlike her friends, Vyzen was downing shot after shot of some bourbon she found in the back of the refrigerator. The bag and the doll sat on a table in front of them, and one by one they said what they thought was in the bag. The guesses ranged from gold coins all the way to a secret recipe for the ultimate potion.

They continued drinking and guessing for a couple of hours until the guesses got so far out of the box that they were just stupid. That's when Vyzen grabbed the bag and dumped the contents onto the table. Upon seeing what fell out, the women gasped and fell backwards against the wall. Lying there on the table in front of them were two blue eyeballs with a puncture wound on each side. The optic nerves were still attached and helped keep the eyes from rolling off of the table.

"Who's are those?" one of the girls asked.

"You know goddamn well who those belong to," Vyzen yelled unable to keep her anger under control. "That son-of-a-bitch not only ripped them out of the High Priestess's head, but he had the nerve to take them as a trophy! What kind of Satan spawned demon does a thing like that?"

"Who is he?" the girl asked.

"I think I know who it is and where he is going to be tonight," Vyzen said as she took her Vodou doll and rubbed it all over the doll from inside the box. "I have been reading how to use these. As I understand it, if I rub it onto something he touched, then the curse will only work on him." She held the doll up in the air and she watched as it glowed with its new power.

"Gods, spirits and demons," she prayed, "please grant us this wish. Allow us to use your blessings to seek revenge on he who harmed one of your loyal subjects." Suddenly, the glow got immensely brighter, and the doll was becoming hot...not quite hot enough to burn her flesh but extremely close. She grabbed the eyes, put them back in the bag and left. The others wanted to help, but Vyzen forbid them from going with her and, because of her state of mind, they listened.

Vyzen walked down Canal Street toward an arena by the Superdome. There

195

were hundreds of people standing in line waiting to get in. She looked around and noticed that most of the people were dressed in black leather, and she was sure that she saw more than one smiling with perfect sets of vampire teeth. She couldn't tell if they were fake or not but she knew that, in New Orleans, there had to be a culture of vampires, and that was something she didn't want to get involved with. Suddenly, she saw what she was looking for, a poster advertising the "New Vodou Priest—Kenneth LaTrobe."

'That's the son of a bitch I'm looking for," she said to herself as she reached into her purse, took the vial she got from the shop and drank it. The drink immediately increased her focus and her anger to such a point that she would have killed an innocent if they tried to stop her from what she was planning to do.

Tickets were $25 just to get in the door. If she wanted to meet LaTrobe, it was going to run her another $100. "Not worth it," she said, "even if he was going to be around to meet anyone anyway." Vyzen bought a ticket and went in. Her seat was all the way in the back which was the perfect place to be for what she had to do. By the time the rest of the audience was seated she noticed that, besides about a dozen people in the row down below her, the back of the theater was empty.

Twenty minutes later the entire place erupted into screaming and roaring applause as a choir entered the stage and began doing some old Vodou chants and songs. The entire place went crazy with people dancing wild dances and shouting as loud as they could. It was almost as if Vyzen had walked into a frat party, but with religious music.

Vyzen took the doll out of her bag and started stroking it gently as if she was trying to please the spirits. "Please allow me to complete what I have to do," she said to the doll. "It was an injustice done to your most avid follower. I pray that you will help me in my quest." She felt a rush of warmth starting within her and eventually enveloping her entire body. She took this as a blessing from the spirits, and that made her feel better about her task.

A few minutes later, a voice came over the speaker system. "Ladies and gentlemen, allow me to introduce the new leader of the Vodou sect in New Orleans...High Priest Kenneth LaTrobe," it announced as the crowd whipped themselves into a rabid frenzy.

"What in the hell...," Vyzen said to herself. "I have never seen anything like this."

LaTrobe entered the stage and stood perfectly still before the audience. It felt like forever before he started speaking. Of course, the crowd was so loud Vyzen couldn't hear a word he was saying, but she could imagine every word. However, she could hear one thing—the old woman's voice coming from deep in her head. "Child, do not kill the man who did this to me," she said. "Although he did me wrong, he is a living being, and he shall not be killed in my name. Please obey my words and you will be rewarded."

Vyzen had no idea if this voice was real or something her mind was creating. But she quietly stood up and walked from the hall and into the closest women's restroom. Once there, she checked to see if she was alone. The room was clear of people, so Vyzen locked the door, took a black candle from her purse, set it on the sink and lit it. The flame was strong, and it burned a beautiful bluish black.

"Praise be the spirits," she said. She knelt down on the floor. It was very uncomfortable, but it had to be done. Once she was in position, she took a scroll from her purse and read it out loud, "I light thee with only hate in my heart. Only with revenge in mind, I give thee light to aid my rage into the direction of thee I hate. Make Kenneth LaTrobe see the hurt he brings me, make him feel the pain I feel. Remove the hate from my heart, and all the pain he has brought me. Move it toward the more deserving. All he has done, he shall now see. I will seek my revenge times three. As this burns, your pain shall begin, and all you brought me, now shall end."

Suddenly, she heard a scream, actually 300 screams all at one time, coming from the inside of the arena. She blew out the candle and ran out of the restroom, up the steps and into her aisle. The audience was pretty much gone by the time she got to her seat. She watched while LaTrobe rolled on the floor screaming in pain. "What's happening to me?" he screeched.

Vyzen watched for a moment and then, ever so slowly, she took the Vodou doll from her purse. She sat there for a minute looking at it and looking at the man on the stage. The words of the High Priestess echoed through her thoughts. She must not kill the man no matter what, so she reached into her purse and brought out a long needle from a small pouch.

"LaTrobe," she yelled, "do you truly want to die for what you did to Her Highness? She does not wish that for you."

199

He looked up at her—his face still in dark grimace of true pain. "Who are you?" he screamed.

"My name is Vyzen," she yelled back." Renounce your claim on the throne!'

Without even thinking, he shouted that he would never renounce his claim.

"Renounce your claim," she yelled even louder. Again he refused, so she took the needle and shoved it through the eyes of the doll. Vyzen watched in shock and amusement as LaTrobe's eyes both exploded. "Renounce it!"

"Never !" He screamed as he stood up and grabbed his eyes. But before he did, Vyzen could see that his eyes were not ripped out as the queen's were. They were nonexistent.

"Renounce it !" Vyzen yelled as she took the needle and shoved it through both of the doll's legs. LaTrobe fell to the floor and blood poured from his wounds. The last thing she did was to drive the needle into the center of La Trob's throat. He tried to scream and scream loudly, but, despite his effort, he was unable to make a single sound. Vyzen wanted to do one other thing, but she knew that she had done enough in order to make the man to suffer even more than the queen had suffered. He was a quivering hulk on the floor, but he was still alive just as Her Highness had requested.

Vyzen went from the arena back to the shop. The door was unlocked, so she walked in. She found the queen sitting in the backroom just as she was when Vyzen left hours before, except that now her head was bandaged.

"Come in, child," she said. Vyzen did as she was told. She walked in and knelt down before the queen.

"Has it been done?" she asked.

"Yes," Vyzen replied.

"Is he still alive?" she asked as she touched Vyzen on the head to make sure she was there.

"Yes, he is still alive," Vyzen replied

"I am very proud of you, Little One," she said with a smile. Then she lowered her head and whispered a prayer. Actually, it was softer than even a whisper. Vyzen could hear the air moving, and that was about all. The queen finished her prayer, raised her head and removed the bandages. Vyzen fell back on the floor with her eyes locked on the face of the queen. The old woman's eyes were back in place. She looked as if nothing had ever happened. "Kneel before me," Her Highness said. Vyzen got up off the floor and knelt down as she was told. "Vyzen," she stated, "you have proven your loyalty and respect for your queen. I have no children so, from this moment on, you will be my daughter and will serve as my princess."

Vyzen lowered her head and swore her life to her new mother.

The queen died almost five years ago now, and Vyzen took over the shop which she still keeps the way the old woman liked it. She has also taken over the throne to the Vodou sect in New Orleans. As Vodou Queen, she has taught hundreds of people the art of Vodou and the ramifications of using the dark side. She also has had a little girl of her own whom she is raising to take her place when her reign is over.

The city of New Orleans is still the capital for Vodou in the United States, it is just a lot better since black magic was banned.

The shout still goes up through the city, long live Queen Vyzen, and it will for a long time to come.

County Road 136

I lived in a little town, in the Pennsylvania mountains called Allegheny Heights, it is a small town of about 12,000 people. The thing is a lot of very, very strange stuff happens in the area. I have always heard about it, but I have never been fortunate, or maybe it's unfortunate enough, to see any of it...Until that one night.

For some reason, I don't know why, I took my dad's old El Camino. They were out of style back when they were being built, and I think the reason was that no one could accept a car/truck hybrid, but now they are considered to be classic and fairly expensive to own...If you can find one.

Anyway, I picked up some of my friends and we went out drinking. Now, I didn't get drunk.. Maybe I should have, but I was the responsible one. Before you think, what I know you are going to think... How responsible could I be if I was driving around in a stolen car? Actually, I didn't really steal it, I just went for a ride without telling Dad I was going.

It was after 3:00 AM when we finally got done drinking, dancing and getting into trouble, so I dropped **(them)** off my friends and took the back roads home. County Road 136 was usually quiet in the daytime and dead as hell at night. I mean the road is nearly 45 miles long, and you would be lucky to see another car, an animal, or anything else from the time the sun went down until it came back up in the morning, I liked it because it was so lonely.

That night I admit that I was buzzed...I mean really buzzed, but when I turned on that road, I was right. There was nothing to be seen or heard for about a half a mile until I saw this really hot girl standing on the side of the road. I slowed down to take a look. She had red hair, blue eyes, blood red lips and really sexy long fingernails. Oh man, the way she was dressed...Jean daisy dukes, a halter top that was decorated with blue roses and a pair of snow white cowboy boots. There were two things that really caught my eye and those were her boobs. Now, I am good at guessing, and I estimated them to be 38DD.

Definitely enough to feed every baby in the county with some to spare, so of course, I pulled over and offered her a ride. She climbed in and took the seat next to me. *God*, I thought, this had to have been the luckiest night ever.

"What's your name sweetheart," I asked. I watched as her mouth moved, but I couldn't hear a sound, I could tell from her mouth that her name was Marianna, "It is nice to meet you Marianna," I said as she moved closer to me. "Where do you live?" I asked, as her body came so close to mine I felt as if she was climbing inside of me. She just shook her head no, and she pushed on the gas pedal.

I felt the engine roar and the tires catch on the dirt road. It was such a glorious feeling, one I had never felt before, I watched as the speedometer went from zero past the speed limit, and shooting on up to 85 miles per hour. It was hard to see, but when my headlights caught something it was nothing more than a blur.

I kicked her foot off of the gas, and she lifted her leg and wrapped it around the stick shift. I was already in third gear, but she used her legs to shift into forth and then fifth. I tried to lift her leg from where it was, but she took my arm in her hand and quickly but gently slid my hand deep between her legs. It was strange, yet exciting. Where she should have been warm and damp...Her body, especially that area, was ice cold.

"What is the hell," I yelled. Again she moved her lips without a sound. "What in the hell is wrong with you?"

She smiled and stroked her fingernails up the inside of my thigh. Of course that made me tense up and my foot pressed harder on the gas pedal. I watched as the speedometer flew past 90 and all the way up to 120 miles per hour. I knew this road well and I knew that in less than five miles I was going to hit Dead Man's Curve.

EVERY little town has a place they call Dead Man's Curve. Usually it is just there for parents to scare their kids with to make them drive safe when they first get their license but in this case it was true. Since the 1950's, more than a dozen kids died trying to take that curve at too high of a speed.

By the time all of that went through my mind she had moved her hands up and she had them wrapped around something I really don't want to talk about...at least not in mixed company. I brushed her hands away...stupid me...and got back to driving. It was a mere two minutes before I was going to be at Dead Man's Curve.

I was still going at over 100 miles per hour. I tried putting on the brake but, although they slowed me down, it was not going to be enough. She looked like she was screaming (but not out of anger for me) pushing her hands away. She was scared for her life. There was a little over 200 feet when I reached down and grabbed the gearshift. Even between her legs I was still able to shift from fifth gear into reverse. I had never heard a sound like that before in my life...metal ripping against metal, the engine and the transmission fighting for ultimate power and the tires screaming as they skid on the rocky road.

"Oh my God," I screamed as I noticed gas and transmission fluid spraying out of the back end of the car. One small spark from the bumper and I was leading a huge ball of flame and it was getting closer very fast. Then, just as suddenly as it formed, the flames shot into Heaven and all that was left were some small weeds along the side of the road. They were burnt badly but my one thought was. Well, at least it ain't me!

The car stopped right at the entrance to Dead Man's Curve. I wiped the sweat from my brow and looked over to where the girl was. The door was wide open and she was gone.

Since I tried and couldn't get the car to start I called my friend and asked him to come out and get me. I knew that he would say yes but I had no idea that it would take him an hour to get there. All I could to do was look around the area. On the side of the road was a cross. It was so white that it was easy to see even at night. There was a list of everyone who had died because of the curve. All in all there were 17 names listed. The oldest was 1943 the newest one was 1998. I looked carefully at each one. There, about half way down, was the name Marianna. She was killed there in 1962.

Needless to say I lost my buzz in a big hurry. Could it have been....no, I thought that would be impossible. Still, I drive that road at least three times a week and I have never seen her since but I wonder, if I had kept control of my car maybe she wouldn't have left. But, I will never know unless some night I am trashed and I happen to see her standing along the side of the road. I might just pick her up and try again...after all...how many times do you find a really hot girl just standing there waiting for you?

Life after

I've thought so many times about what happens when you die. Hundreds of TV shows tell you what could happen—what you see and what you will feel. To tell you the truth, I thought all of that was a crock of shit, until that day two years ago, when I died in the hospital.

I was in an accident out on Walnut Creek. I was driving my car, a 1970 Gremlin that I bought and restored. I remember that the road was wet, slippery and covered with a lot of leaves that from the hundreds of maple trees that lined the road. I wasn't being as careful as I should have, as my mind was on a concert I was going to see that night. The Rolling Stones were playing at the Entertainment Centre, and somehow I managed to get second row seats. That was amazing, since the concert sold out in less than a half hour.

I was about fifteen minutes outside of town, and I was doing sixty-five in a forty-five mile per hour zone. Unfortunately, the car that was coming from the other direction was doing the same.

I had just dropped down into the

Walnut Creek valley when I saw something on the side of the road. I'm still not sure what it was—an animal or whatever. So I slammed on the brakes, and that made me skid sideways on the road and stop. Unfortunately, this happened on a blind curve, and, when the other driver came into the valley, he never saw me. He hit my car broadside. I remember hearing the crash and feeling the car flip and roll down the side of the road and into the creek.

Now, this is all speculation: I assume that an ambulance came and took me into the hospital. I couldn't see anything, but could hear what people were saying, but at that moment it sounded like a foreign language. It was like I was in another country. I was aware of where I was before and this certainly wasn't it. While I was in the ambulance, being rushed to the hospital, I could tell, by the tone of the paramedics' voices that something was way wrong with me. I knew that they were worried, but like I said I couldn't understand what was being said, but the tone of their voices was strong with emotion.

I am sure I made it to a hospital, and I am also sure that I was hooked up to bags of fluid, IV drugs and as many machines as they could find.

Suddenly I saw a young girl standing at the foot of my bed. She was dressed in white with a gold sash and a deep violet cloak. Her hair was blonde, almost white and her face looked like a white marble bust I had seen when I was at the Human History Museum when I was a kid. I didn't know her. I had never seen her before.

"You have to come with me," she said. I noticed that her eyes expressed sadness and yet they were peaceful.

I looked down at her, and suddenly I felt a sense of calm, but that was tempered with confusion and curiosity.

"Where are we going?" I asked.

She placed her hand in mine, and said, "It is time for you to stop suffering and live in eternal peace and love."

It felt as if I didn't have a choice. I held her hand tightly as I sat up and stepped down from the bed. It was then that I looked back and saw at least a dozen doctors standing around the bed where my body lay. I jerked my hand from hers and walked over to the bed. I looked down and saw that my shin was ripped to shreds and the doctors working desperately to try and keep me alive.

"Come with me," she said as she once again took my hand. "We have to leave." She turned and we walked out of the room and down the hall, finally stepping through a door and into nothingness.

"Where am I?" I asked.

"We are in the Netherworld," she said as a small light appeared in the distance and with it was the most beautiful music I had ever heard. The light got closer, and the music continued. It became most relaxing and even more peaceful.

The light was finally right before me. The girl stepped into it still leading me by the hand. I was not afraid and nor was I any longer curious about what was happening to me. The music was also louder than it had been, but there was none of the pain from the blaring music that I had when I went to concerts.

"Charlie, come here," a voice said from further in the light. It was a familiar voice, but one that I had not heard in over thirty years. There was only one person who ever called me "Charlie," and that was my mother. "Charlie," the voice said again, "come here. Walk toward me."

I strained my eyes, but I could not see my mother.

"She is not as you remember her," the girl said. "When a person rises, their soul takes the shape of their living bodies at the moment when they were the happiest."

When I looked again, there before me stood a woman no more than twenty-five or twenty-six years old. She had a brown black hair and the darkest brown eyes I had not seen in a very, very long time.

"Mother?" I asked not quite knowing what the answer would be.

"Yes darling," she said as she walked up, held me tight in her arms and gave me a loving kiss. "I have been waiting so long to be able to hold you again. I want you to know that I have been watching over you for your entire life. It was the saddest day of my life when I passed over."

"Where are Dad, Grandma, Grandpa and Aunt Sandy?" I asked.

She pointed over to a crowd of people who were standing a few feet away looking at me. I recognized my dad, Grandma and Aunt Sandy. Grandpa looked familiar from photos I had seen when I visited Grandma when I was a little kid. I went over and talked to them and even told them all about my life. I could understand what everyone was saying, except for my grandpa. He was speaking German…a language that I could not understand but I still have an idea that he was happy to meet me.

The girl walked over to me, tapped me on the shoulder, took my hand and said, "I am sorry but we have been here too long."

"What do you mean?" I asked as we lifted off of the ground or whatever you call what we were standing on. She didn't answer. Then, within a few minutes, we were passing through clouds. It was actually beautiful. "Are we in Heaven?" I asked again without an answer. Finally, we left the Earth's atmosphere and a few minutes later we passed by the moon. "Where are we going?" I asked in an amazed tone.

"I cannot tell you where you must go," she said in a very, very sweet voice. It was even sweeter than when she spoke to me in the hospital. It was actually extremely relaxing, which is what I needed at that moment.

Ahead of us were the planets, stars and galaxies, but also ahead of us was a bright white light that appeared to be maintaining its distance from us no matter how fast we were traveling. By the time we actually caught up and entered the light, we were beyond the edge of the universe. There were no more stars or galaxies. Ahead of us was just one large blue green planet with white clouds floating in its atmosphere.

As our feet touched the surface, the girl told me that this place was my destination, and it would be where I would spend eternity. I looked around and I saw cities, farms. mountains and beaches. "Welcome home Charles Cope," she said. "May your eternity be all that you wish for."

I knelt down to feel the soil. As I did, the girl started walking down a narrow path. I looked up and yelled to her," Thank you very much," I said, and then I asked her a question. "What is your name?"

She looked at me and raised her hand in the way a Catholic priest would do when he is blessing his congregation. "You know my name already, Charles," she said. "I am called God in your reality, but I go by other names in other places."

I looked at her and my mouth stopped working. I just stood there looking and trying to figure out what to do or what to say, but nothing was working.

"Follow the trail along the beach," she said. "It will lead you to a Heaven that you make for yourself."

215

I did what she told me to do. I walked down the trail, and there it was…the house I had always thought of when I was a kid. Flowers, vines, bushes and a really large brick and wood wall surrounding it. It had everything I had ever wanted and so much more. When I went inside, I found that there were games, TVs, musical instruments and a bed that lifted ten feet into the air. It was…truly my fantasy house.

However, just as I stepped into the house and saw all that it had to offer, I felt a sharp pain in my chest. I dropped to my knees wondering what was going on, and where you go if you die in Heaven. Then there was another pain and another and another. I lay on the floor praying and asking God to come and help me. I wanted to live there. I did not want to die there. She never did come to my aid, but my prayers got stronger as the pain increased.

Finally, feeling as if I had lost all of my strength, my eyes closed and I felt a hand grab me and throw me off on the surface and into the, pardon the wording, heavens. I felt like I was flying, I could not see where I was going, but it felt so familiar. I was being ejected from Heaven, my soul was being sent to Hell. I had no idea why. I had lived a good life; I never lied, cheated or stole from anyone. I never killed. I didn't even eat meat, so why would I be going to Hell.

I passed stars and planets as my soul sped up. The pain was still there, but my mind was on other things. I didn't want to go to Hell, but there was no way to stop it.

Finally, the biggest pain of all wracked my soul. It was unbearable, but I was still moving. Suddenly the pain tore me apart, and the next thing I knew I could hear voices… Human voices, I heard someone say that the heart massage and the zapping saved my life.

I opened my eyes, and there was no fire and no smell of sulfur. Instead, there was a cool breeze, a bright light and the distinct smell of alcohol and medical disinfectant. What in the hell was going on? My mind was wandering, trying to understand what was happening. Then it hit me. I wasn't sent to Hell. The pain I had felt were the doctors working to save me. I was alive.

Sometime later I was in my room, and my wife and kids were standing beside the bed. She was holding my hand and crying. I woke up and saw so many smiles. Even the doctor—the one who massaged my heart—was there. "You are a lucky man Mister Cope," he said. "We nearly lost you."

You know, I have never told anyone this story. I doubt that anyone would ever believe it anyway, but it had to be told, and maybe, just maybe, there will be someone who may believe it. In my mind, it was true. I saw the Heaven that the Church has always been telling us about. Believe it or not, it is a paradise. I just hope and pray that maybe next time I might be able to stay.

Rakshasa's Jar

My grandmother owned a small antique shop down on Cedar Road, right across from the chocolate shop where I spent most of my time when I was a kid. I also spent quite a bit of time at Grandma's store and then when I turned twelve, something happened to turn my life topsy turvy. My grandmother simply disappeared without a trace.

The police searched for four months, but to no avail. She was gone, and the thing was that she left without closing and locking her store up.

I was one of the first people back into the store after she disappeared. There was a ton of dust covering everything. Most of what she sold in the shop was purchased from estate auctions all over the state, but despite her efforts, very few things ever sold. The residents of Allegheny Heights were just not the kind of people to be interested in old things. The few sales she made were to out of towners who were just passing through, saw a quaint little shop and decided to stop in. Thank God for her pension or else she would have most likely starved to death.

Whenever I was out of school for the summer, my mom and dad always gave me the job of doing an inventory of everything that was in Grandma's store. I hated the job as I had other things to do, yet luckily I could usually find some freaky things that Grandma would let me take home. So, even though I hated the job, I just loved going through everything she had collected.

When she disappeared, and it was obvious that she wasn't coming back, I was given the job, once again, of doing a complete inventory of her shop. Of course there were a huge number of ivories, silver and even a few gold thimbles, antique cameras and some paintings by artists no one ever heard of. Yeah, they were beautiful pictures, but not really anything anyone would buy.

After inventorying everything in the main part of the store, I finally made it to the backroom where she kept the big stuff and her pottery. There were antique appliances, old

Grecian statues and one thing that caught my attention—a huge Chinese ginger jar. It was beautiful, without a chip in the porcelain, and it was inscribed with Chinese characters surrounded by naked mermaids. Grandma had put a price tag on it of $12,000 saying that it was more than 1,000 years old. The strange thing was that it had a gold amulet dangling from the lid. I decided to grab both and take them home. It took all I had to move it. It was over three feet across and weighed what I thought was a ton but I rolled it as best I could.

When I got home, my mom and dad were out at their jobs, so I rolled the jar up the one step at the front of the house. I had always complained that I wanted a bedroom on the second or even third floor, but at that moment, I was so happy that we had a single floor house. I could barely contain my pleasure because it actually got a lot easier to roll once I got it into the house and finally into my bedroom. I stood it in the corner of the room. Luckily the lid never came off, and there was no discernible damage to it, so I covered it up with one of my blankets and went back to the shop to finish the job of counting things.

I got back home about 8:30 that evening. After quickly eating my dinner, I rushed into my room, closed the door and locked it behind me; I did not want anyone to know about the jar until I was ready to show them.

"What are you doing in there?" I heard my mom yell from the living room.

I had to think quickly, so I pretended to be on the phone. I knew that she had already walked from the living room to a spot near my room. "I'm working on something with a friend of mine," I said.

"Working on what?" She asked.

"We have a game tomorrow down at the youth center, and we're planning our strategy so we'll win," I replied. She knew that I played baseball, so that sounded to me like a perfectly good story that I knew would work.

"Okay," she replied. "I won't see you when you wake up so good luck with the game." I knew that excuse would work. Hell, her and dad never went to my games so they wouldn't ever know that I was fibbing.

I walked over and pulled the blanket off of the jar. It was so shiny and perfect I could not believe it. I wanted to remove the lid, but it was on too tight; it wouldn't budge. I tried heat, Vaseline, hair oil and I even went down the hall to the kitchen and even got some cooking oil to try. Nothing I tried worked.

Finally, I grabbed it with a rubber glove my mom used to clean the bathroom with and twisted as hard as I could. I heard a grinding noise as the lid moved just a bit...just enough to let me know that it was working. The more I tried to loosen the lid, the louder the grinding got until it was so loud that I was sure that Mom and Dad could hear it. At long last my efforts were working. The lid was moving farther and farther until it came off in my hand.

My heart was beating so loud and pounding so hard that it felt like it was going to come out of my chest.

I sat down on my bed. My body was shaking. It was almost orgasmic, but since I was only twelve and certainly didn't like girls, and was a virgin, I am using that description not going by my lack of experiences. Yes, it was orgasmic. It took a long time for all of the excitement to leave my body.

Ten minutes later I still had the lid in my hand. The inside was covered with mother of pearl, and the rainbows that came from it were absolutely beautiful. There was also a symbol painted inside—a Chinese symbol that I was curious about and I knew I had to get translated to find out what the jar was used for.

The next morning, I did rubbings of the symbols and decided to them to a college down in Pittsburgh. I had heard from some of my friends that they taught Mandarin there, so they might be able to translate the symbols for me.

After a one and a half hour bus ride I went into the administration building on the campus and saw the name Dr. Lin May Chou, Professor of Chinese Culture and Language. I found his office in a nearby building and went in. My luck was fantastic that day. There he was sitting behind his desk grading papers or something.

"Doctor Chou?" I asked in a voice that was nervous and yet excited.

He looked at me. "Yes boy, I am Doctor Chou," he said with a smile on his face. "How may I help you?"

I took the rubbings out of my pocket and handed them to him. He got a stern look on his face as his eyes darted back and forth over the symbols. "Boy, where did you get these?"

"I got them from a ginger jar I found in my grandma's antique shop," I said. "They are all over the thing surrounded by naked mermaids."

His face turned white as he looked at the rubbings. "This is the name of Rakshasa, an ancient Chinese demon," he said. "My guess is that the ginger jar is not a ginger jar at all."

I looked confused. After all, I had seen many of these in Grandma's shop. This one was bigger, but otherwise, no different from the others.

"I think it is some kind of burial jar," he explained. "They used them back in China to bury the spirits of those who did evil—even more so when the spirit was a demon, which is what Rakshasa was—one of the worst there was."

"Why?" I asked. "What did he do?"

"He did everything he could to disrupt funerals, torture and steal souls both living and dead and so much more," he said. "Basically he was a total bad dude!" Then he asked me if I could bring the jar to his office.

"I had a hard time getting it home," I said. "I live in Allegheny Heights. I don't think I could get it down here." He assured me that would be no problem. He would get a few of his graduate students to come to my house and pick up the vase. I told him when my parents were working and set up a time for him to send the students over.

"When you get home," he said in a very strict voice, "do not look inside the jar. Put the lid back on and seal it as tight as it was when you found it."

I didn't ask why. He was way too serious to answer any questions I may have. So I promised to do as he said, and started to leave for home. Before I left, I told him that I wanted to be there when he opened it. He reluctantly agreed and I left.

I got home a few hours later, and the jar was still right where I had left it. Everything looked the same, except for one thing...there was a strange glow coming from the opening of the jar. It was a kind of blue, but, yet, not blue. It looked almost as if someone had mixed a deep black with navy blue.

Yeah, I was curious. How could I not be? I was a boy, and that had to be the strangest thing I had ever seen. Instead of looking inside, I did as the professor had instructed. I placed the lid gently on top of the jar and pressed down to seal it to the rim. When I finished that, I twisted and pulled on the lid to make sure that it was sealed tight. It was.

That night I didn't get much sleep. I kept dreaming about Rakshasa. In my dreams, he would dig up the graves of the dead, and hide the bodies many miles away so that they could never be found. Or I would see him going into children's hospitals, leaning over the children and sucking their souls right out of their young bodies, leaving them for the nurses to find on their next rounds. No matter what the dreams were, they came to me every time I closed my eyes, and they were as realistic as if I were there watching what he was doing. Everything he did was worse than the thing before and all of them combined made a story that even Wes Craven could not conjure up.

I woke up sometime around seven. I looked at the jar and then around my room. My gaze stopped when I glanced over at my bedroom mirror. There on the mirror were scratched the words 我希望我的鑽石. Now, I could never read Chinese other than to order General Tao's Chicken, but somehow mysteriously I knew what those words said…"I want my diamond."

I looked at the words for a moment and then thought it best to write them down so I could show the professor when I got to his office.

My folks left around 8:30 and the students showed up sometime around ten, so it was safe for them to take the jar and haul it back to the university. I'd be damned if they were going to leave me behind. As they were closing the back of the truck, I ran and jumped into the front seat.

"You aren't supposed to go with us," one of them yelled.

I was determined that if the jar was going, so was I. "That jar isn't going anywhere if I can't go with it," I yelled right back at him.

"The professor...," he started to say.

"The professor said that I could be there when that thing is opened, and I want to make sure I am," I yelled.

Now, I am not sure if I won the argument or if he just gave up, because he mumbled something, got in the truck and we started off for Pittsburgh. It wasn't that far away, but it seemed farther because the students didn't speak and they had some hokey religion program on the radio that promised salvation for anyone willing to give the pastor $1,000 and it sounded as if he was promising sainthood for a donation of $2,500. It was all a crock of shit. I knew it. Pretty much everyone on the planet knew it, but the moron driving the truck took it as gospel.

We finally got to the university, and I walked with the guys as they carried the jar inside. Dr. Chou was there waiting. He was dressed in a white lab coat with some kind of velvet gloves, which I assumed was to keep his body acid from touching the surface of the jar.

"I did some more research on those rubbings," he said. "It is definitely a jar that the ancients thought would hold the spirit of the Rakshasa. It got lost sometime around 900 years ago and ended up in a couple of independent collections over the year. There were always stories, but nothing was ever proven and no one was allowed to study the jar until now, thanks to you." He then looked at me and asked me if I had looked inside. Of course, I said no since I hadn't and I didn't tell him about the message or the glow from inside the jar—at least not then.

They put the jar on a low table. The students started making their own rubbings and measurements of the cap, noting the circumference and the weight. Then Dr. Chou started playing around with the lid. It was holding tight and he was trying to force it open. Both he and his students were trying. They were groaning hard, and breathing harder than people normally should. The lid still didn't move.

"Move away," I said as I walked up to

the jar. They all backed away, and I put my hands on both sides of the lid and gently squeezed as I turned the lid right for a few millimeters and then to the left and it came off easily. I stood there holding the lid as the others just glared at me for knowing how to do it. As soon as the lid was off, however, they all gathered around, but not too close, to see what was hidden inside. Dr. Chou was the first one to actually look inside.

"Give me a flashlight," he requested. One of the students brought one for him. He turned it on and then he stuck his head almost all the way inside the jar before he had any kind of reaction. When he finally did have one, we watched him back away. I was sure that he did some kind of dance. He said he didn't, but the way his feet were moving it could only have been a dance. It took him like ten minutes to calm down. When he did, we heard all about what he had seen.

"Canopic jars," he said with a voice still straining from the excitement. "It has a half a dozen of them in there. I saw them I saw them all. They are jade—the deepest green jade I have ever seen and the lids are carved in the shape of different dragon heads. One looked as if it was just freshly carved...like maybe sometime in the last couple of years."

"My grandma has had that thing for five years I think," I said. "I just know she never put it out for sale, and no one was allowed to touch it."

The doctor went back over to the jar and started removing the canopic jars one by one, setting them on a nearby table for more research on what their engravings said, and why they were in a ginger jar, in the first place. Then, while he was removing the last jar, he let out a yell so loud it almost shattered the jar. "I found it," he yelled. "I found it!"

"Found what?" I asked.

"I had heard about it since I was a freshman in college; I always thought that it was just a legend but now it is here in my lab. I cannot believe my pure luck," he was yelling as he ran around the room while kind of bouncing off the walls. Then he did something I'd never expect. He ran over and gave me a hug.

"What is it?" I yelled as I backed away from him. He reached into the jar and felt around for a second before he pulled his hand back out. When he did, he was holding a large diamond—a black diamond—that was blacker than even the midnight sky out in the desert.

Smiling, he said as he held it out, "This has got to be the Diamond of the Gods. It is said to hold all of the powers of the Chinese gods when the ancient peoples turned against them."

"Doctor," I said in a very nervous voice, "there was a message on my mirror this morning that said, 'I want my diamond.'"

Suddenly his face turned white—whiter than even the clouds outside.

"When you opened the jar did you see anything strange?" he asked.

"Not when I opened it," I said.

"When then, boy?" he yelled at me. "When did you see it?"

I stood there for a minute. Yes, I was getting more and more scared with every second that passed. "When I went to close it," I said nearly in tears. "There was a glow and a mist that came out of the top and disappeared. I thought it was just dust from the jar being so old."

"Glowing dust?" he asked. It was easy to see that he was getting angry with me.

"I didn't know," I said. "I never opened anything like that before."

"Do you know what you did?" he asked. "Do you?"

I just stood there shaking, but I managed to shake my head enough to let him know the answer. I didn't know what I had done.

"You released Rakshasa. You let the stealer of souls out into the world."

Just then, the ginger jar shattered, and the canopic jars flew across the lab. No one was near it, and no one could explain how or why the jar broke, as we were all too busy trying to keep the canopic jars from breaking. We gathered all six of them, placed them on one of the smaller tables and wrapped them in bubble wrap just to make sure that they were safe.

They didn't notice at the time, but a door in the far wall slowly opened. Now, I knew that door had a squeak in the hinges, I had come through that door earlier, but now it was totally silent. The doctor and his assistants were busy picking up the shards of the ginger jar while I was looking at the carvings in the canopic jars. They were beautiful, to say the least. For a young boy, the images were just too fantastic for words. I just stood there and stared for probably fifteen minutes.

In a split second, a figured appeared out of empty space. It was ghastly to look at. It had ruby red hair surrounding an oriental face.

Horns protruded into the air, and each sent a sulfuric smoke into the air. Its hands were burnt so badly that it was hard to call them hands. They were more like paws with claws that measured at least six inches in length. Its eyes...I will never forget those eyes. They were glowing green...the same green as the canopic jars, but they were transparent. Standing there, I could see right into the back of his skull. The funny thing was...he didn't have a mouth...at least not one that I could see. That, despite everything else, was the freakiest thing about this creature.

"Can you see that?" I asked in a strangely calm voice. I know I should have been freaking out...you know, running around, yelling, but I didn't feel that. Everyone in the room looked at me as if I was crazy, and pretty much in unison they all asked, what in the hell I was talking about. I pointed and said, "Right there! You can't see that...thing standing there?"

Dr Chou told me that there was nothing in the room, but I knew better, I could see it. Whatever it was it walked by me without even looking at me. "What are you doing?" I asked as it walked farther and farther from me, and toward the table where Dr. Chou and the others were working. "What are you doing?" I asked again in a firmer voice and, again, it just ignored me. Dr. Chou shouted back to me that he was looking at that diamond he found in the jar.

When he said that, I could see the creature's ears perk up so at that moment, I knew who it was and what it was after. "Rakshasa," I yelled as loud as I could and as I did, it turned slightly and its eyes locked onto mine for just a second before it turned back to Dr. Chou. I saw in its eyes that it was the creature that was locked in the jar for 1,000 years. It was the demon, and it wanted that stone.

"Boy, will you be quiet for just a moment," Dr. Chou yelled back at me. "I have to be extremely careful with these artifacts. I will be just a few minutes and then I will talk to you."

As soon as he finished talking, Rakshara stood directly behind him. He wasn't in the posture he was when he walked in. It was almost as if I was looking at a cat stalking a bird. It was like watching a cougar hunt a small mouse and the mouse didn't know it was behind him.

"Dr. Chou," I yelled. As I did, Rakshara

raised his hand and just one of his claws touched Dr. Chou on the shoulder. I watched him fall, Dr. Chou was gasping for breath and he finally withered into dust. The creature just smiled. It was almost as if I heard it laughing.

"No," I screamed as I ran over to the doctor. He was just a pile of dust. No skin, no muscles, no bones...just a pile of dust.

I looked up and saw Rakshasa reaching toward the table. I guessed that he was going to steal the diamond and take all of the powers locked inside of it. I also knew one thing: since all of the students had taken off when Chou collapsed. I had to be the one to get the diamond, and I had to do it fast.

It seemed as if it didn't notice me any longer if it even had noticed me at all. I was able to move around without it looking at me, to see where I was, or what I was doing. So I slowly walked up to the table. The creature just reached for the diamond, when I stepped between it and the diamond, snatching the stone from the table and running across the room with it. It was then that Rakshasa really started watching me.

It started toward me at a pace a lot faster than it was using when it walked in. It was growling loudly and that kind of sounded like a dragon. Its mouth was fully open and, for the first time, I got to see into its mouth. Yeah, there were long sharp teeth on the edges, but the rest of its upper mouth was filled with barbs that looked a lot like a collection of the sewing needles my grandma used to sew with. Its eyes, I will never forget its eyes. They weren't the color I'd seen earlier. They were glowing brightly, and the color was something that I could not comprehend. It was truly terrifying.

I just stood there holding the rock. It was a lot warmer than it was when I picked it up, and it kept heating up until it was burning the flesh from my hand, but, even through the pain, I kept my hand wrapped tightly around it. Rakshasa was no more than ten feet away from me when the pain got to be too much for me. By now, I could smell my flesh burning, so I opened my hand, and the diamond fell to the floor shattering into a lot of pieces. As it did, Rakshasa screamed in pain, and he backed off.

At the same time, I looked and saw the canopic jars shaking. They made such a loud noise that I fell to the floor with my hands covering my ears, but that didn't help. The noise was so loud that even through my hands I was sure that my brain was going to explode.

I could feel blood flowing from my ears and nose. The noise got louder and louder until I heard a number of small explosions. I counted six in all. Then I heard something strange...six voices in different languages and they were all yelling at the creature.

I looked up and I saw several people. One looked like the pictures in my history book when we were studying ancient China. Another was dressed like a Greek soldier, and yet another looked like a knight who had stepped out of twelfth Century Britain. The last figure I saw was a woman dressed in modern day clothes. She looked familiar, but I wasn't sure who she was.

"Demon," the knight said. "Turn and face us." He stood still except that he had pulled his sword and was holding it before him. The others did the same, except for the woman who was unarmed and just put on a show of her bravery. "You have kept us captive too long," he continued.

The creature turned toward them and started running right at them. It was growling louder than it had when it was after me. It seemed to have one thing on its mind, and that was to kill everyone in the room.

The knight stepped forward and shoved

his sword into the chest of the creature. He twisted the blade while the others used their weapons to slash and stab the creature. Rakshasa swung its claws back and forth trying to slice his enemies. Its bites were so powerful that I could feel them way across the room. But its claws and teeth never found a target despite several attacks. The knight stabbed the creature again, and again, each time deeper and more powerful than before. Finally, the creature fell onto the floor, and, after one more terrifying growl, he turned into dust and was blown away in a breeze.

I crawled out of my hiding place and ran over and kicked the last bits of dust across the room.

The knight came over and handed me his sword. "You were brave, son," he said. "Not many men would have been able to do what you did. Live your life with honor and you will be as brave a man as you are a boy." I stared at the sword. It looked very familiar. I thought about it for a minute and then I looked again at the sword and then at the man.

"Your majesty," I said as I looked at the sword and back to the man. "Are you…?"

"Yes," he replied.

"And is this…?"

"Yes boy, you are holding my sword," he said. "It has served me well, and I want you to have it to protect you and help you be brave throughout your life." He walked back over to me and touched the sword. He smiled and talking to the sword, he said, "Protect this boy as you have me." Then he just turned and walked away. I knew at that moment who I had been talking to. I had met King Arthur of Camelot.

One by one, five of the six figures faded away until I was standing there facing the woman. She walked up to me and said, "You do not recognize me, do you?"

I told her that I had never seen her in my life. She was young and dressed like a woman right out of World War II. Yet, she had an accent that I had heard all of my life.

I looked closer at her and looked into her eyes. "Grandma," I cried out excitedly as she wrapped her arms around me.

Then she whispered in my ear telling me that, yes, she was my grandma and that she was going to a much better place now—that she had been saved. I knew I should have been sad, but I actually felt happy for her. Then she told me one other thing before she, too, faded away. As soon as she was gone I looked over, and somehow, the ginger jar was back in one piece. I didn't see it happen, but it did. Just another mystery of the jar, I guess.

I took the jar back home that day. I made sure that the lid was always kept far away from the jar. I had it for about a week before I talked to my mom and dad and told them everything. I also told them about my visit from Grandma and what she had told me. We took the jar to the post office, packed it up and sent it to a museum in Hong Kong. Of course, the lid was sent separately. We didn't want to take any chances.

Me, I still run that little store my grandma owned. It is doing well, and I always keep a picture of my grandma on a shelf behind me. That way I know that she will be there if I need her.

I forgot about Excalibur. I still have it after all these years. It is stored in a velvet-lined box, in my bedroom, and when I have a son, he will get Excalibur when I die. I hope that it does as good for him as it did for me.

The Recipe for Passion Pie

One of my favorite, strongest memories from when I was a kid was of my grandma Nellie. She was one of those women who nobody was quite sure of...smart, very attractive for someone her age and, somehow, when she died last year, she had been married for more than seventy years.

Now, she was spicy to say the least. When you were around her, you never dared to state your opinion. You had to wear your hair and clothes a certain way and, god forbid, you ever, ever disobey her. She had a switch and man, did she know how to use it! The thing was it wasn't just us kids who had to obey the rules; her whole family had to do the same. I have no idea how, or why, Grandpa put up with her, but he did!

The thing is she was always working in the kitchen. No, it wasn't that she believed the way to a man's heart is through his stomach. Honestly, but she couldn't cook well. Let me put it this way, she made a roast beef and it ended up being a chocolate cake. But one thing she loved was collecting recipes.

After she died, being her only living relative, it was up to me to clean out her house. It was actually fun. I found such strange things. I could not believe that Grandma would ever own things like that. My favorite was a shrunken head. She mentioned it a few times when I was younger, but, you know how grandparents are, I never quite believed her. Anyway, I found it and now it hangs on the mirror in my '67 Mustang. It cuts down on hitchhikers. After all would you accept a ride from someone driving with a shrunken head in the car?

The last thing I found was her recipe file. It was really great seeing how they cooked in the "olden days." While looking through the little box of recipes, I found one called Passion Pie. I took it with me and decided to have my wife make it. I stopped at the store on the way home to pick up the ingredients. Most were simple—peaches, apples, cherries... but there were some I never heard of.

I ended up in a specialty shop where I found the Blood Sauce (a mixture of sweet sugar cane, cherry juice and the juice of a blood orange), Witches Cauldron (vanilla and rye with a touch of fire water) and there was something I couldn't pronounce, but I got it anyway. I didn't even want to know what was in that.

When I made it home, I handed the recipe and the ingredients to my wife, and she just smiled. It was an evil smile, but I just let it go as she rushed into the kitchen.

Now, before I go any further, I have to let you know that she and I had been having problems—bad problems. They were so bad that I seriously wished that the Gates of Hell would open and suck her in. I am sure she thought the same about me.

She was in the kitchen for a couple hours. I could smell dinner, and it smelled good. Roast turkey, mashed yams, stuffing with country gravy and of course that Passion Pie.

We barely talked through dinner. That was nothing new. Honest to God, we never spoke. Finally, the dessert came. I took the first bite. All of a sudden, I felt every bit of anger fade from my body. By the time I had finished that piece of pie, I wanted nothing more than to take my wife, rip her clothes off and make love to her over and over again. And, lucky for me, she was okay with it!!!

After that, every weekend, no matter what else we ate, we always ended dinner with Grandma's Passion Pie. My new love for my wife never ended, despite the fact that she hadn't changed. She was still a bitch, but I loved her more than the day I met her.

I didn't know it—no man does—that recipe for Passion Pie is known to every woman. It is passed from generation to generation for use in just such a circumstance. I just happened to be the fool who found the only written copy and, instead of posting it for men to learn from, I handed it to the enemy and she made me fall in love with her all over again.

Damn that pie!

About The Author

R.e. Taylor was born in Akron, Ohio in 1956. He began reading at the age of three. He began writing at the age of six, writing children's stories and basic poetry. Years later he developed into writing and illustrating comic books, as well as writing more advanced fiction stories.

As an adult R.e. Taylor has written three novels, several plays and movie scripts, a collection of short stories, as well as more than 400 poems which will be published in a two book set called "Serenity" and "Confusion".

He is also a photographer and a video cameraperson and is the owner manager of television and movie production company "Xanadu."

He is also a highly skilled professional painter and quilter, and was also the producer/director of the highly acclaimed local music rock show "Erie Rocks."

For many years he worked as a

journalist and theatre critic and has always been interested in paranormal activity and is a well-known ghost hunter advisor and trainer.

Although he writes light stories and poetry, Taylor prefers to write dark imaginative stories and poems that leave his readers amazed at the diversity of his writing.

The reason he prefers the dark is that writing dark material "is so much fun because you are not under the constraints of having to make a character behave properly."

However, despite his dark side, some stories and many of his plays are lighthearted, especially his comedies with interesting characters and laughs from start to finish. In fact the reader and audiences are always in for a unique experience.

R.e. Taylor's credo is to "Make the impossible plausible." He is pleased when someone writes to tell him that a twist he had written into a story surprised them as every word he writes strives for that goal.

www.ingramcontent.com/pod-product-compliance
Lightning Source LLC
Chambersburg PA
CBHW072221170626
46813CB00003B/1036